A Murder at Greenbrier

D.M. MacDarvey

PublishAmerica
Baltimore

First printing

At the specific preference of the author, PublishAmerica allowed this work to remain exactly as the author intended, verbatim, without editorial input.

ISBN: 1-4241-2453-0
PUBLISHED BY PUBLISHAMERICA, LLLP
www.publishamerica.com
Baltimore

Printed in the United States of America

Dedication

To my wonderful husband, Dave, for having the patience and love to bear with me while I made my dream of becoming a writer a reality. Also, to my children, Penny, and all of those who had faith in me.

Delores,
I hope you
enjoy the book!
D. M. MacDarvey

Acknowledgments

For my mom, Millie, who gave me the love of a good mystery and the ability to solve a case, which to this point has remained unsolved.

It was a balmy afternoon for November in Pennsylvania. Usually by this time, Greenbrier had already experienced its first snow. This was something that Katie definitely was not looking forward to, after last year's record-breaking cold spell, along with snow that was measured in feet instead of inches. It was in the sixties on this beautiful day, and the sun warmed Katie's face as she made her way home from work. The now brown withered leaves, which just a month and a half ago had adorned the trees with their vibrant hues and brilliant shades of yellow ochre, crimson, and orange, now crunched under her feet with every step she took.

She was deep in thought as she made her way down the tree lined Greenbrier Lane, which was considered the center of their little village, when a voice brought her back to her surroundings with a sudden jolt.

It was Doctor Campbell, Greenbrier's local doctor, whose voice had brought Katie back to reality. He was in his thirties and was well over six feet tall. His sandy blonde hair, which always appeared as if he had showered and then had hurriedly run his fingers through it, was in its usual state of disarray. This gave him a distinctly disheveled appearance that definitely added to his charm. His darkly tanned face would light up from the flash of his smile, and Katie had liked him from the first day of their meeting one another. It was not only because of his deep compassion for those that were under his care, but also because of his easygoing nature. He never wore suits and ties, but would dress in jeans and tee shirts, or flannels for this time of year. He always said that he did not want his patients to get the white coat syndrome from his looking too doctor-like.

This certainly would not be a problem, Katie thought. The first time she met him, he was walking down the hall of the hospital, and Katie had erroneously thought that he was the new maintenance man. She had stopped him to inform him about a plugged toilet in room three that needed his attention. He had found this so amusing that he never let her forget it.

"You sure are a millions miles away, Katie," he said in his easygoing manner.

"Hi, Doc." Katie blushed as she always did when she was caught off guard, which she had to admit was quite frequent these days.

"You caught me daydreaming again," she said as she looked into his blue eyes, which were the color of sapphires and crinkled at the corners when he smiled.

"I bet I can guess where your mind was, Katie." He had stopped and turned towards her.

With a little embarrassed laugh she said, "Oh you can, can you?" She could feel her face getting redder under the intense scrutiny of his gaze.

"It was on murder, wasn't it?" The smile that crossed Doc's face could have lit up a room.

"Now how did you know that?" she blurted out. She knew that he was insightful, but how could he have known that murder was exactly what she was thinking of? Was he psychic or something? As they continued down the sun-dappled lane, Katie thought once again that he was one of the most intelligent people she knew.

He gave her a knowing little wink. "Everyone has heard that the ACDC has invited you to join their ranks, so what else would you be thinking of, besides murder? By the way, I would like to be one of the first to congratulate you."

"I'm not in yet, but I'm certainly going to give it my best shot," Katie said with a little laugh that escaped her perfectly bowed lips.

As they walked side by side down the lane, her long strides easily keeping up with his, he asked her, "Okay, let me guess, what was on your mind?" He gave her another knowing smile." Were you trying to plan the perfect murder, or are you, as I imagine attempting to solve one?"

"I'm trying to solve a murder alright, Doc, but murder in my opinion is never perfect." He stopped once again and turned towards her. He was studying her face intently as she made this statement.

"What about all of the murders that go unsolved in the world? Wouldn't you consider them perfect murders? I mean you have to admit that there are so many murders that there are no arrests for."

"If there is one thing in life that I am absolutely sure of, it would be that there is no such thing as the perfect murder," Katie said again as they continued down the lane.

"Of course there are murders that have gone unsolved for a variety of reasons," she said as they made their way along the lane, the leaves crunching under their feet. "This I believe is sometimes due to sloppy police work, or it could be because the accused can afford to have a battalion of overpaid lawyers to get him off. It could also be because no one even realized for one reason or another that a murder had been committed." She was watching for his reaction as she said this.

"In most cases," she went on, "I believe the reason is that the murderer in all probability just got lucky, which I believe happens more times than not. I also believe that for anyone that has the ingenuity to come up with the almost perfect murder, there is a counterpart out there somewhere, with the ingenuity, or serendipity to stumble upon the truth."

He gave her a long searching look as she finished speaking.

"The way you consistently solve the murders at our Halloween parties, I would think, that if anyone could solve a real life murder, it would be you, Katie. I mean you could give the rest of us a chance now and then, don't you think?"

"Everyone has the exact same clues as I do to solve those cases, Doc. I just seem to have the capability of grasping things that others fail to notice." Katie said this in the matter of fact way that she was well known for around the little village.

"You certainly do that," he said, his eyes crinkling at the corners as he smiled at her. "I hadn't even begun to guess the true identity of the murderer at this year's party when you blurted out who it was."

"Well, that was rather easy compared to what the ACDC wants me to attempt to do so that I can join them."

"And just what murder do they think our little sleuth can solve that has remained unsolved to this point?"

"They want me to solve the Simpson – Goldman Murders."

"You mean the O.J. case?" He gave a low whistle. "You sure have your work cut out for you, don't you?"

"It would certainly seem so," Katie said, a worried look crossing her face.

"Just remember you really don't have to solve the case, you just have to make them believe that your theory could be how the murders actually happened. If anyone can do this I know you can."

"I wish I had half the confidence in myself that you seem to have in me, Doc."

"You are extremely bright Katie, and I know that if I were ever on trial for murder, you would be someone that I'd want on my side trying to prove my innocence. I definitely wouldn't want you trying to prove my guilt."

As they came to the end of Greenbrier Lane, they stopped to have a bit more conversation. Katie promised to bring him some homemade chocolate chip cookies to work the following day, knowing that they were his favorites.

"I'd certainly appreciate it, Katie. Nobody makes cookies as good as yours. After all Becky isn't known for her cooking abilities." He gave a little laugh.

His wife was a lovely young woman who had given him two adorable little girls, now four and five years old. She enjoyed taking care of her family and being with them, and she was the perfect mom and wife, but in reality, she really wasn't a very good cook.

"As pretty as Becky is, I'm quite certain that it wasn't her cooking abilities that first attracted you to her," Katie said, looking up into his face.

"No, that's for sure, but it really wasn't her beauty either," Doc said in the most sincere way. "It was actually her deep compassion for everyone and everything around her that really first attracted me to her."

"Really." Katie gave him an inquisitive look at this last statement.

As they stood there, Doc smiled at the look that crossed Katie's face.

"The first time I ever laid eyes on her, Becky would not have been considered beautiful by too many men other than me. She was kneeling along the side of the road by a drainage ditch. It had been raining heavily since morning and she was soaked clear through to her skin. Her hair was hanging down in wet strands around her dirt smudged little face, and her mascara had begun to run down her cheeks in little black rivers," he smiled at the memory. "Her futile attempts at wiping the tears from her eyes smeared it even more, and as she stood there she looked like a half drowned baby raccoon that had fallen in to a mud puddle." Again, a warm smile crossed his face, and Katie knew that he was remembering just how she had looked that very first day.

His voice softened as he recalled the details of their first meeting. "She had found a tiny kitten that had somehow fallen into the ditch, and she was desperately trying to rescue it from certain drowning. By this time, the water was rising minute by minute in the ditch from the torrential downpour. I had stopped to help her, and together we managed to retrieve the kitten from its precarious predicament. I will never forget her standing there holding the sopping wet kitten against her chest. She was trying to warm its frail, shivering little body, with her own body heat, tears still streaming down her dirty little face. As she stood there trembling, she began to stammer how I was her hero. I knew at that very instant that this was the woman I would marry." A warm nostalgic look crossed his face as he told her the story of how they'd met.

"She really is an amazing young woman." Katie was thinking of how this would be exactly something that Becky would do. They were truly a perfect couple.

"Speaking of spouses, how is George doing these days? It's been a long time since I've seen him."

"He's just fine. I'm going to make an appointment for his annual physical with you, as soon as he has a day off."

"Tell him that he can come in anytime. You sure are a lucky woman, Katie; George is one of the best people I know."

"I guess we've both been blessed in that department, haven't we."

"Truer words have never been spoken," he said with a smile that Katie thought could cure any ailment.

They said their goodbyes, and Katie made her way down the brightly lit lane, which she had walked down so many times before. She was headed for the public library, having decided that she needed to refresh her mind on some of the details of the Simpson case.

Katie was thinking as she continued on her way that she really was very fortunate indeed. She had what she considered the almost perfect husband. He was tall and handsome, with broad shoulders that appeared as if they could carry any burden. He had thick brown hair that he kept trimmed to perfection, along with his mustache and beard. His hazel eyes, with their flecks of gold, were truly the windows to his soul. Even after all of these years of marriage, if he caught her eye across a crowded room, she could feel the hot flash of desire well up inside of her, erupting from the very depths of her being. His hands were calloused from the many years of construction work that he had done, yet when he touched her, they felt as soft as silk. She loved her husband with all of her heart, and she knew that the feelings were mutual.

She always said that she had the almost perfect husband, since he still did those husband things that get under every woman's skin. For instance today it had taken 15 minutes to sweep the living room carpet before Katie left for work, when Good Old George, who really wasn't old at all being only forty nine, decided that he was going to go hunting. Katie was happy that he had decided to take a day away from his contracting business to have a little R & R for once. He had gone to the garage to get ready, and it just so happened that after he got all of his hunting gear on, including his mud-caked boots from his last venture, he decided that he needed to get a few more essentials from the house. In through the house he came making a path of dried mud through the entire house, not just once, but twice. As she said, except for a few little things, he was the perfect husband.

Good Old George was how all of the locals fondly referred to him. George was the most likable person anyone could imagine. He helped everyone, and everyone liked him for his easygoing nature. He also was the most straightforward, honest man that Katie knew.

Katie was also well-liked around the village. Not for being kind or easy going, though she was, but people liked her because she was tenacious and somewhat eccentric. Some people may view these traits as character flaws, but Katie thought they made her personality what it was. She never backed away from anything, and she would fight for what she thought was right with everything she had. George often jokingly said that she was the only woman he knew that would go to the gates of hell just to spit in the devil's eye.

It had all started a few weeks earlier on Halloween night, Katie's favorite holiday. She loved Halloween, because not only was it her dad's birthday, but she had always found that it was a holiday that could be enjoyed without the hassle other holidays entailed. It did not force you to go above and beyond, as most holidays did. You did not have to buy gifts, and then have to add return slips, so that the recipient could return them for something that suited their fancy better than the gift that she had presented to them. There were no huge meals to prepare, which would be consumed in the matter of minutes, leaving her with the mess to clean up. What she always loved most was that you could be what, or whomever you wanted, and no one thought you too peculiar. It was also the anniversary of George and her first date; this made it very special indeed.

The townspeople of Greenbrier always had a huge Halloween party, which was held at the Greenbrier Estate. Jeremiah Greenbrier, the founder of their little village, had built the mansion in the early 1800's. Every Halloween, the Woman's Auxiliary that Katie belonged to would transform the great hall of the mansion into Dracula's haunted castle. It was complete with coffins containing skeletons or vampires. Mechanical witches they strategically placed about the room gave cackling laughs as they stirred their magical potions in black caldrons, all the while chanting spooky little spells and incantations. Black bats, which appeared so real that they sometimes frightened Katie, would fly over the witches' heads from lengths of fishing line attached to the ceiling. Cobwebs hung everywhere, and spiders, with eyes glowing from the tiny red lights that they painstakingly wired them with, seemed to watch for unsuspecting prey. The webs would lightly brush Katie's face in the gloomy darkness as she passed under them, making the hair on the back of her neck stand straight up. Ghosts made from sheer white gauze performed ghostly dances above their heads. While the thin wires that they were suspended from made it appear as if they were flying about the room by themselves, their long white shrouds fluttering in the breeze from the open windows.

They had even purchased several fog machines that would fill the huge room with an eerie haze, which made it appear as if a heavy mist had fallen over the entire room. This always reminded Katie of the cemeteries in the old horror movies from her childhood. The haunting sounds, blood curdling screams, and howls that came from the surround sound speakers in the great hall would have been enough to frighten Dracula himself, Katie thought to herself.

The screams and squeals from the children and adults alike was testimonial of the fine job that they had done transforming this elegant room into such a frightening place. People came from miles around and paid a nominal entrance fee, which the auxiliary donated to the hospitals pediatric unit, just to have the chance to be frightened half to death.

They would play games with the children, such as bobbing for apples, an old Halloween favorite. The haunted ghost walks were enough to scare even the bravest of heart. The pumpkin-carving contest was always a great success, Greenbrier having some rather talented artists in the area. They would do their best to carve cats and spooky faces in the pumpkins, which would then be displayed on the brightly decorated tables. When the orange and purple lights that adorned the elaborately decorated room were turned off, the great hall would be illuminated by the glow from the candles inside of the pumpkins. Prizes were awarded for the most creative jack-o'-

lanterns, and the contest had become quite competitive over the last couple of years.

In recent years, they had included as part of the festivities a murder mystery night for the adults. After the party was over, all of the young people went about trick or treating in the neighborhood. The adults would remain at the old Jeremiah Greenbrier estate, trying their best to solve the mystery that they were given. The mystery, which was thought up by one or in some cases, all of the ACDC members was generally quite difficult. The Greenbrier ACDC, which had started back in 1916, was comprised of the most brilliant residents that Greenbrier had to offer. The Greenbrier ACDC stood for The Greenbrier Arm Chair Detective Club, which over the years was shortened, to the ACDC. The members always attempted to stump the partygoers with a murder mystery that they felt would be difficult to solve, and they would start to prepare for it months in advance of the big night.

This year, as in the two previous years, Katie had solved the mystery in record time. In fact, this year the mystery was so easy for her to solve that even she thought she had jumped to the wrong conclusion.

The mystery they were presented with this year had been very difficult indeed. It was about a very rich old woman, who met her demise at a dinner party she was having. The main character in this murder mystery was Mrs. Pennybrook, who was played by Ann Crook. Ann was one of the newest members of the ACDC, having lived in the village for approximately 3 years. After discovering that she had been murdered, it was their job to figure out just who had done the dirty little deed. There were many suspects, as there always were in the murder mystery.

Mrs. Pennybrook's new husband, played by Ann's real-life husband, Tom, was on top of most of the amateur sleuths' suspect list. From the clues that they were given at the dinner party it would have seemed likely that he had done it.

Other suspects on the list included the maid, played by Brenda Cormick, a long-time member of the ACDC. Old Mr. Thomson, who was the elder member of the club, played the butler. There always seemed to be a butler lurking around somewhere in these mysteries. While Colonel Simons, another of the clubs elders, played her prodigal son.

Katie had figured out that the murderer was the maid, who it turned out was actually a niece that the murdered victim had not seen for years, and who she had willed all of her money. There had been so many clues during the mystery dinner that Katie had found the solution quite simple indeed.

After Katie had discovered the identity of the murderer, she was asked by several members of the ACDC to join them in the library. They were so impressed; they said with the deductive reasoning that she had used to solve the case this year, that they wanted her to join their prestigious club. Katie was so elated by the prospect that she could have jumped for joy. She could think of nothing that she wanted more. She had been waiting patiently for the club to ask her to join them, and now that it had finally happened, she was temporally speechless. She soon found her voice, however, and readily agreed.

So ecstatic was she at the prospect of being in the click that she scarcely paid attention to the daunting challenge that they gave her. They wanted her to prove who had murdered O.J. Simpson's ex-wife Nicole and her friend Ron Goldman. Most of the town folks still believed that O.J. had done this horrendous crime and had gotten away with it, even after all of these years. When the realization that she would have to prove that it was O.J. himself, or someone that no one else had even considered, came to her, it was like a kick in the stomach. How could she prove what dozens of trained professionals in that line of work had failed to do?

Yes, Katie thought, her life was almost perfect; the only thing hanging heavy on her mind at this point was having to solve a murder that to this point had remained unsolved. How would she ever accomplish this? After all, what did a nurse know about murder? She was very good at solving TV murder cases and those that the ACDC tried to baffle them with at the annual Halloween parties, so she would have to give it her best shot.

She was in fact a trained observer; you had to be to be a nurse. She would just do what she did when solving any of the mysteries that had come up before her in the past. She would think it through and base her theories on the facts. Once she put her mind to it, she was sure that she could come up with a reasonable solution to solving two murders that had remained unsolved for so long. After all, she kept reminding herself, she only had to come up with a theory about the way that they could have happened. She didn't have the overwhelming task of proving, it without a reasonable doubt, as had the prosecutors in the actual case.

As she made her way down the lane, she kept telling herself that if she ever hoped to get in to the prestigious Armchair Detectives Club, this was going to be her only chance to do so. Everyone in the small community of Greenbrier wanted to be in this club. However, only the very few that could use their brains, or as Hercule Poirot would say "their little gray cells," to figure out mysteries would be admitted into the club or the hallowed halls of the Greenbrier Mansion, where they held their meetings. There were rules to gain a seat in the ACDC, such as you had to be to convince the group as a whole that you had figured out how a real-life mystery could have been committed. If you could convince the group that your theory was plausible, then you gained a place amongst them.

Over the years, most of the group had been challenged with such mysteries as the Jimmy Hoffa disappearance, the Lindbergh kidnapping or any other mystery that had been unsolved thus far or in which the suspect had been acquitted. Even if there had been a successful conviction, if you could prove that your theory was just as likely as what the real detectives had figured out, the ACDC would sanction you into their realm.

Katie was in a quandary as to how she would convince this group of armchair detectives that O.J. had gotten away with murder. Of course, since there were never any other suspects in the murders, her best bet would to be to try to prove that O.J. did it. She would also have to prove how he had gotten away with it. The LAPD and all of the prosecutors on this case had failed to prove how he had done it.

Though absolutely convinced that he had committed the murders, they had failed to prove it without a reasonable doubt. Now little old Katie Scarlett Adams yes she had been named for Scarlett O'Hara from her mom's favorite movie of all time "Gone With the Wind," had to prove how the murders of the last century had been committed. She found herself in the ominous position of having to succeed where everyone else had thus far failed.

She would have not only to get the details back in her mind, as they were no longer as clear as they had been when the murders occurred, but also to prove to a group of exceptionally intelligent people that she could be correct in her assumptions.

Katie walked down to the Berry Patch where the public library was located. When the town had been founded back in the1800's, this had been where the locals would come to pick berries for their jams, jellies and homemade wines, mostly the later, she believed. Of course, there had not been any berries here for the last 75 years, but the name remained an icon.

She was headed for the library with one thing on her mind. She must find out all of the information about the case that she possibly could. After all, it had been a worldwide case. People from all over had watched the case as it unfolded on TV. It was as if it were a soap opera, being made up as it went, just for their entertainment.

It had been a spell binding-case, in which the prosecution and defense teams were the magicians. They both had used so many slight of hand tricks to attempt to get the jury to believe their theory that it really was like a magic show.

As she walked deep in thought, she could not help but notice once again what a beautiful day it was for November. Her nostrils picked up the acidic aroma of burning leaves wafting towards her from Mr. Grant's yard. This had always been one of her favorite smells next to freshly mown grass.

As she entered the library, a nostalgic feeling overtook her. She had spent so many hours here as a child; it was almost like a second home. Whenever she was late getting home from school, the library was the first place her mother would come looking for her.

Old Mrs. Hicks, the librarian, sat at the huge front desk. Katie still remembered how as a child she would have to reach up high to place the books she was borrowing on the desk. Now the desk was waist high to her, but Mrs. Hicks had never changed. Katie guessed some things never did. She had looked eighty back then just as she did now, Katie thought. The deep creases of her face told of the many years she had been an avid gardener. Back when Mrs. Hicks was young, they did not know about the damaging rays from the sun and how it could make the skin age. There were no sun blockers to block the harmful rays, as there were now. Her white hair, always neatly done in a braided bun at the back of her head, was the color of newly fallen snow. She used the bun as a pencil holder so that she always had one on hand when she needed it. Katie had often thought that her hair would hang down in beautiful white waves that would reach her waist, if she ever released it from the securely intertwined braid. Her hands, now gnarled with arthritis, appeared as if she could barely lift some of the books that she loved so much. Though she had a rather stern appearance, she was one of the gentlest, loving people that Katie had ever met.

Mrs. Hicks motioned Katie to the desk when she saw Katie enter the library.

Katie gave her a smile and Mrs. Hicks returned it.

"Katie, you do know that the Agatha Christie book you borrowed is now a week overdue?" She admonished her as if she were still a little girl, but there was a hint of a smile at the corners of her little wrinkled mouth.

"Oh Mrs. Hicks, I've been so busy lately that I completely forgot about returning the book." She could feel a lump of guilt form in her throat as it always did under Mrs. Hicks's stern gaze.

"You know that you will be charged ten cents a day for every day that you keep it over the two-week borrowing time, Katie."

"I will bring it back in the morning and put it in the deposit box along with the fine. I will do it on the way to work, if that's okay?"

"That will be fine, dear," Mrs. Hicks said, her little wrinkled face trying to be stern even though Katie could detect the underlying smile.

Katie had always been so interested in books that she rarely brought them back on time even as a child. The library had probably purchased its first computer with the proceeds from all of the fines that she had paid over the years.

Mrs. Hicks smiled at her, and Katie knew that she was being dismissed from any further lecture at this time.

Katie made her way to the newspaper archives, which were located in the bowels of the library, to see what she could find out about the O.J. case. It was a very dimly lit room even though this section, which had previously been used for storage, had just recently been added to the library. Everything was on computer these days, much to Mrs. Hicks chagrin. The radiance of the computer screens cast an eerie glow to the surroundings.

She sat there for hours acquiring as much information as she could from the computers. After she had searched through all the news articles she could find, her eyelids growing heavy from the task, she made her way back up the beautiful wooden stairs to the main floor of the library. As she was ascending the stairs she passed Tom Crook, he was heading for the archives.

"Hi Tom. Wasn't it a beautiful day?"

"Hello, Katie," he said brushing by her.

Katie could see by his manner that Tom was in a hurry to get downstairs, so she did not pursue any further conversation with him.

As Katie departed the library, she flashed a warm smile towards the front desk where Mrs. Hicks sat stamping books. Mrs. Hicks gave her a little nod, and Katie left remembering how she had grown to love books because of this wonderful woman.

Mrs. Hicks had told her as a child, "Katie, when you read a book your mind is in control of how the characters are portrayed. You can picture everything the way you want it to look in your imagination. On the other hand if you watch a movie, someone else is in charge of how things appear," She had said these words in her quiet librarian voice.

"Have you ever read a book and known exactly how someone should look by the description in the book, and when you watch the movie you were disappointed because the character didn't look at all the way you had imagined?"

Katie had said that this was very true.

"Katie, my girl, don't ever settle for that. Keep your love of books by reading and using your own imagination. When you read you can do or be anything you want. You can travel the world without leaving the security of your own home. Remember, Katie, you are only limited by your own imagination," she had said with a fond smile.

Katie had taken these words to heart. She loved reading and the knowledge reading had given her, and she probably read more books than anyone else she knew. Katie not only appreciated the words she read, but also thoroughly enjoyed the hours of entertainment these words had given her over the years. On the other hand, Good Old George was an avid TV watcher. Sometimes he was a bit jealous of Katie's preference for reading over sitting with him in front of the TV. This had been especially so when they had first been married, but over the years, he had come to understand how much pleasure reading gave her. Nowadays, he rarely said anything when she picked up one of her favorite books and curled up on the couch in front of the crackling fire that they continually kept going in the beautiful stone fireplace on cold winters nights. He just smiled and went off to watch TV.

Leaving the library, she walked back down Berry Patch Lane. She was glad she had refreshed her mind of the details of the murder and the subsequent trial. Katie remembered a great deal more concerning the murders, after her visit to the library. The trial had been televised, and she had been an avid watcher, as had everyone in Greenbrier. Most had taped it while they were been at work. She had not had to do this. She had been at home at the time with her mother, who was convalescing after a surgery. She had been at home for almost the entire length of the trial and rarely missed a day of it.

The thing that she had refreshed her mind on, were some of the details about the glove. That was going to be how Katie got into the ACDC. She would attempt to prove that O.J. had been the one wearing that glove the night of the murders, and that he had dropped it on his own property. Katie would have to prove that Mark Fuhrman, no matter how arrogant she thought the man was, had not framed O.J. by planting the glove found at O.J.'s home after the murders. Katie thought it went without saying that if the prosecution could have proven without a doubt that it was O.J. and no one else, who had dropped the glove on his own property that fateful night, it would have been a slam-dunk case for them.

Katie had not wanted to believe at first that O.J. had committed these horrendous crimes. After all, he was one of football's greats. On the other hand, even though it was later divulged that Mark Fuhrman had made racial slurs that greatly bothered her, she could not see him ruining his long police career over trying to frame O.J. for murders he had not committed. Katie had been pulled back and forth over these doubts for the entire trial. She had desperately tried to figure out whether O.J. had dropped the glove that was later discovered on his property, or indeed whether Mark Fuhrman had planted the glove where it was eventually discovered behind O.J.'s home.

Ever since the beginning of the case, Katie thought, she had the threads of how to solve it in the back of her mind. She would have to weave these strands of suspicion into a plausible theory, as if she were a weaver attempting to use a multitude of different colored threads to make a completed pattern. She was certain she was missing a vital clue that would unravel the mystery, but Katie believed that the case could be solved quite simply if she could only put her finger on it.

The case revolved around the glove. This was obvious to almost everyone. The people who thought O.J. was guilty were sure that he had dropped the glove on his own property. The ones that thought him innocent were sure that the police, in particular Mark Fuhrman, had planted it there.

Katie knew that it was just out of her reach, hiding in the far corner of her thoughts. She had to try her best to reach in to the recesses of her brain and bring it to the forefront. She knew that she could find the answer, but at this point, it remained illusive.

Katie had always believed that as humans we tend to make things much more difficult than they really are. When people are given a riddle that they're desperately seeking the answer to, they usually muddy the waters with a great many things that don't fit. She always thought people tended to think that the riddle was so difficult, as to be unsolvable. By doing so, they can't see that sometimes the simplest explanations are the correct ones. Katie had always gone by the old adage KISS, "keep it simple stupid." More often than not, this worked for her because her mind was not overwhelmed with unimportant facts that hid the truth.

One bit of information that she had forgotten but that had returned to her after her visit to the library was that the glove did not fit when O.J. had tried to put it on at the trial. After seeing numerous photos of O.J. with the glove halfway on his hand, she remembered that they had made O.J. put a rubber glove on before attempting to put on the leather glove.

As a nurse, Katie was someone that wore rubber gloves all day long. She knew it was virtually impossible to pull even a large glove on over a rubber glove unless you really tugged at it. When she had seen this charade being played out on TV, she had tried to accomplish this by trying to pull a leather glove that was her size over a rubber glove. It was almost impossible. The glove being made of rubber prohibited the leather glove from being pulled on, until she yanked on it with all of her might.

Why would the glove that O.J. attempted to put on not fit? It should have gone on if O.J. had pulled with any effort the way that Katie had, if it were his glove, she thought. It was obvious to anyone who had watched the courtroom antics that this glove looked very different from the one found at the murder scene. This glove had been discovered hours after the first glove had been found, but it should not have appeared so different from its mate. This glove was withered and wrinkled, and in much worse condition than the murder scene glove. Why did it appear so much smaller than its mate? Katie believed that it must have been dampened at some point and then shrunk as it dried. This had always puzzled her. How would the glove have gotten wet? It could have become damp by the dew, or the blood could have made it damp enough so that when it dried it could have shrunk to some degree. From all of the pictures she had seen, the glove appeared as if it had shrunk at least two sizes.

Now Katie thought, what would have happened if O.J. had been given the other glove, the one that had been found at the murder scene? Katie believed that if this had been the case, he could have pulled it over the rubber glove without too much difficulty, since, Katie believed, this glove was much closer to the original XL size that he actually wore. Katie thought that she could find the answer to this question, and it would be much different from any of the other theories that she had thus far heard.

She would have all of her facts in order so that on the night when she went to the Jeremiah Greenbrier Mansion, she would be able to convince the group of the validity of her story. She hoped the fabric of her story would have a completed pattern by then. Katie knew that she could solve this very difficult case, if she could just put her finger on the one illusive clue as to who placed the glove where it was found. She would have to be convincing so that there could be no doubt that what she was telling them was the absolute truth. Katie of course would practice on several of her girlfriends. She would also practice on Good Old George, her three children, and anyone else that would listen to her explanation of her theory.

As Katie entered her yard, she was startled by a voice calling her name from the other side of the neatly manicured hedgerow that separated her property from her neighbors.

"Hello, Katie Scarlett." The voice said again. Katie recognized the voice as that of her neighbor Mrs. Finch.

"Mrs. Finch, you startled me. I didn't see you over there."

"I'm so sorry dear," the frail little voice said.

"Oh it's not your fault, Mrs. Finch. I was daydreaming and I just didn't see you." Katie wondered how her neighbor had seen her coming since her head wasn't even visible above the bushes.

"I was just picking up some twigs from under the hedges, Katie. It is so beautiful today that I wanted to get a few things done in the yard before the weather turns bad."

"It certainly is warm for November, isn't it?"

As they were talking they were joined by Mrs. Finches little dog, Baby. He was jumping up and down, his squeaky little bark becoming more and more frantic as he tried to see who it was his mistress was talking to on the other side of the hedge.

"Well, Katie Scarlett, have you come up with a solution to the mystery the ACDC gave you yet?" Mrs. Finch had to raise her voice to be heard over the barking.

"I have been to the library today trying to do just that." Katie was standing on her tiptoes so she could see Mrs. Finch over the hedgerow.

"Oh I am sure that you will come up with a satisfactory theory my dear. After all you are very good at figuring out mysteries, you prove that every year at the Halloween party."

"This is a bit different, Mrs. Finch. After all this is a crime that really happened, not one made up by the ACDC where all of the clues are right in front of me."

"It will come to you, Katie Scarlett. Of that I am sure."

"I hope that you're right, Mrs. Finch. I have always wanted to belong to the ACDC and I know that this is my only chance to get into the club."

Baby, was putting up such a fuss by this time that Katie could barely hear Mrs. Finch's frail voice. "Well dear, I must go and get our supper ready. I'm feeling a bit weak just now and Baby has to eat at the exact same time every night or his little stomach gets upset."

"Have you been checking your blood sugar, Mrs. Finch?"

"Yes dear, ever since I had that scare back in June, I've been keeping a much closer eye on them."

"If you need anything just call, okay."

"I will dear." Mrs. Finch walked away, Baby following closely at her heels.

As Katie entered her house through the back door, she knew that George had been successful on his hunt. The kitchen was in total disarray, not at all how she had left it that morning.

George came up to her and gave her a huge bear hug.

"Baby you have to see the buck that I got. I think that he has the biggest rack that I ever got." George stood there with the look of triumph on his face.

"Oh, George, that's wonderful." Katie would never kill anything herself, but she was happy for George. She knew the pleasure that her husband got from hunting and he did deserve to take a break now and then from his business.

They went out in the garage to see his trophy and Katie had to admit that the buck was magnificent. George had already processed the dear and the head and hide were all that remained on the garage floor.

"Don't worry about the mess; I'll get it cleaned up before I go to cards tonight. I had to get the meat into the freezer as quick as I could so it wouldn't spoil. It's usually never this warm during hunting season."

Katie had to listen to every detail of the hunt while they ate supper that night. Thank God, she was a nurse so it really didn't bother her too much to hear the gruesome details.

"What are you going to do tonight?" George asked as he was getting cleaned up later that evening.

"I think that I'll try and watch that movie that has been advertised all week. It's a mystery and I have wanted to see it ever since I heard about it."

"You know you'll never stay awake for it," George said as he took her into his arms and held her close.

"I know, but maybe this time I will."

"That'll never happen, Katie. You are the only person I know that falls asleep in movie theaters," George said with a laugh as he gave her another hug. "Maybe you should tape it so you can watch it later."

Katie had to admit that she rarely stayed awake while watching a movie. Her mother use to say she could have her tonsils removed without being put under. Not because she was so engrossed in the movie, but because she would fall into a deep sleep at the very beginning and not wake up until it was over.

As Katie snuggled up on the couch that evening after George left, she could already feel her eyelids becoming heavy. She was determined to stay awake no matter what it took.

Someone, frantically pounding on her door startled Katie awake from her sound sleep. At first, she thought that she was dreaming, but the pounding became increasingly frenzied. Katie's eyes went to the mantel clock and she strained to see the dials. It was only 11 o'clock so she knew it wasn't George at the door, since his card club lasted until midnight. Who could be pounding on her door in the middle of the night? Katie had always felt safe living in Greenbrier, but there had been a rash of burglaries in nearby Simmons lately. Mrs. Finch had informed her of this just the other day.

Katie got up from the couch, heart pounding. George had always told her to call the police if something happened while he was out, but it could be Mrs. Finch or one of her other neighbors at the door needing her for some reason. On the other hand, there was no sense in taking any chances.

Katie armed herself with the handgun George always kept loaded on top of the gun case and eased her way to the door. As she peeked out the small window in the center of the door, she couldn't see who it was that was pounding on it with such force that the door was actually vibrating. Either whoever it was was extremely short, or they were lying on the front porch while hitting the bottom of the door. God, where was her Lab, Sam. If she were there, Katie would feel much braver than she did right now. Katie's thoughts were going a mile a minute. She should probably go to the phone and call for help, but before she could move from the spot that she was riveted to, she heard Sam's deep throated growl coming from the other side of the door.

Katie once again peeked through the small window. She was praying the heavy wood of the door would prohibit the intruder from entering her home. She didn't want to have to shoot anyone, but she would, if that were the only choice she were given. Standing on tiptoes she peered through the small rectangular window, she was trying to swallow the lump that had formed in her throat, but it was impossible. Looking straight ahead, she could not see anything. She then looked down, and the glow of the porch light revealed a sight that astonished her. She was so amazed in fact, that it took several seconds for her mind to register just what she was seeing.

Katie sat in the living room, the darkness that surrounded her should have been daunting after what Katie had just experienced, but instead it surrounded her like a warm, comfortable, blanket. She was waiting for George to return from the card game and it seemed as if time were standing still. She replayed what she had seen repeatedly in her mind. She now had the answer to what had happened on that night so many years ago when Nicole Brown Simpson and Ron Goldman had been murdered. She couldn't believe that the mystery could have been solved in such a serendipitous way, but it had been.

When George returned home, Katie told him exactly what had occurred that night. He first admonished her for not calling someone for help and then he hugged her body tightly to his; she could see the relief in his eyes that she had not been hurt.

"Katie, what would have made you go to the door?" he asked as he held her close to his chest.

"I don't know. At first, since I had been sleeping, I thought that perhaps you had come home early. Then when the pounding reached a fever pitch, I knew there would be no reason for you to be making that much noise. I thought maybe one of the neighbors needed medical assistance, or something." She looked up at him sheepishly.

"Damn it, Katie, why would you even take the chance of going to the door? Sometimes you're just too brave for your own damn good."

"I know it was stupid, but I did take the gun with me," she said chewing her bottom lip.

She knew George was angry with her for doing something that stupid. She remembered the time her oldest son Jay had run out in front of a truck at the grocery store. She had knelt down and grasped him tightly to her breast, relieved he hadn't been hit, but scolding him the entire time.

"You had to be scared to death." George said holding her tightly.

"I was, but once I knew Sam was out there and that she would protect me with her very life, I calmed down."

George reached down and patted Sam's huge black head as she sat there with her soulful brown eyes looking from Katie to George "You sure did help your mom tonight. Didn't you, old girl?" Sam wagged her tail; she seemed very pleased with herself indeed.

Katie tossed and turned half the night thinking about what had happened. She had been given the last thread of evidence she needed to solve a murder that had shocked the world, while being nearly frightened out of her mind in the process. It was amazing.

After what had happened the night before, Katie had come up with the perfect theory as how to solve the Simpson case. Katie, having a hair appointment at the Curl Up and Dye that morning, told her theory to a number of her friends. They were so impressed with what she'd come up with that it gave her the courage to go to the police station to speak to the chief about her theory.

Joe, the chief of police, had been a friend of George and hers for years. She trusted his clever mind and the completely honest way that he had about him. She knew that he would tell her whether he thought that her theory could hold water.

As she entered Joe's office, she was feeling a bit nervous. Not that Joe wouldn't believe her story if she explained it correctly. However, just on the off chance he did not find it substantial, she would have to start again from square one.

"Hi Katie," he said with a warm smile as she entered his office. "What can I do for you?"

"You've heard that I've been invited to join the ACDC, haven't you, Joe?"

"Yes, of course, who hasn't?" He was still smiling.

"I would like to run my theory of the case that they've given me past you and have you give me your honest opinion of it." She was pacing up and down in front of his desk, and he offered her a seat.

"Sure," he said, eyeing her a bit more closely than before." What mystery does the ACDC deem you capable of solving?"

"Well, they want me to prove how the Nicole Brown Simpson and Ron Goldman murders were committed," she blurted out.

"Good God, Katie, you mean the O.J. Simpson case? You sure have your work cut out for you."

"I don't think the case is nearly as difficult as the prosecution and defense teams made it," she said, as she looked him straight in the eye. "I pretty much figured it out from something that happened last night. I just want your opinion on whether my story has validity."

"I'm all ears, Katie," he replied.

She started to tell her story to her friend. At first, she was so nervous that she thought she would never get through it. By the end of her narrative, she was sure she'd been rambling on like some kind of deranged maniac. When she finally came to the end of her story and looked into her friend's eyes, she knew he had believed every word she'd spoken. She doubted that she'd ever been the recipient of such an outright look of admiration in her entire life. She was filled to overflowing with a warm feeling of accomplishment.

"Katie, if you would have been on the prosecution team, and had this theory, there would've been no question as to how the murders happened. Too bad that you couldn't have figured it out at the time of the trial. You would have saved the prosecution a great many headaches."

"Well, it's too late now, Joe. The case has been over for years."

"That's true, but if the prosecution had had your theory at the time, it would have changed everything."

"You really think so, Joe?" she stammered. Katie had been having second thoughts about joining the ACDC after being given such a challenge. As she looked into her longtime friend's eyes, she no longer had any qualms about her decision.

"Yes, I do. I do have one or two questions for you, though."

"Fire away."

After she had answered all his questions, seemingly to his satisfaction, he just sat there staring at her.

"Joe, do you think I can convince the ACDC that my assumptions are correct?"

"There's not a doubt in my mind, Katie. I do have one more question though."

"What's that, Joe?"

"Where will you be holding your celebration dinner after you are inducted into the club?"

This gave her so much confidence that she sat there smiling like a schoolgirl. She knew that Joe believed in her theory as much as she did.

As Katie got up to leave his office, Joe said, "One other thing, Katie?"

"Yes" she said as she turned once again to face him.

"If there is ever a murder in Greenbrier, can I deputize you?"

"Joe, could you please be serious," she said with an embarrassed little laugh.

"I'm as serious as a judge," he said with a look on his face that meant it.

"Since there hasn't been a murder for over two decades in our village, I very much doubt if all of a sudden you're going to need my services, Joe."

"You never know, Katie, you just never know," he said gazing off into space.

She would later remember their conversation, and chills would run through her as she recalled his words.

She left his office walking on cloud nine.

Katie was very confident in her theory. The people she had explained it to would stand in awe, mouths dropped opened and exclaim, "Oh my God, Katie that has got to be the way it happened." She would see the profound admiration that crossed their faces when she finished her narrative. Now that she had convinced Joe, who she admired very much for his great capabilities in solving mysteries, she had very little doubt that she would be successful in her quest for a chair in the ACDC.

As it grew closer to the night, Katie had rehearsed her theory so many times that she had it down pat. Not too many people could doubt the accuracy of what she had to say, she thought. That was before she recalled just who she was up against.

When the big night finally arrived, Katie, as she walked to the podium, had to hold herself back from turning around and running as fast as she could out of the Greenbrier Mansion library. She scanned the faces of the ACDC members in front of her, attempting to read them.

There was old man Thomson, one of the elders of the club. He would be one of the more difficult to convince. The old school teacher had been around so long, that one almost expected him to have personally witnessed the Lizzie Borden trial. He had been given this case for his admittance into the club. He had proven to everyone at the meeting that Lizzie had done the murders for which she had been accused. Everyone agreed that if old man Thomson had been around at the time of her trial, Lizzie would have swung from the gallows.

He was a dapper little man, though his body had become bent and twisted over the years from the rheumatism that afflicted him. He walked with a cane, and his footsteps were so small that he appeared to shuffle rather than walk. The lenses of his glasses were so thick that his eyes appeared to bulge out like those of the huge bullfrogs that made their home in Katie's ornamental fishponds. His favorite attire was an old pin stripe suit that had definitely seen better days. The elbows and lapels were threadbare, and the material had a shine to it from the many years of wear. He had lost so much weight in recent years that the suit hung on him like that on a scarecrow. The weight loss had also made his dentures become so loose that they made a clicking sound when he spoke. He had been a teacher at the local high school for as long as anyone could possibly remember. He had also been Katie's teacher, so this made it even more terrifying for her.

Little Mrs. Finch was also there. What a fitting name for her, Katie thought. No one could have given this little bird of a woman a more appropriate name. Her white hair was always in a bun on top of her head, making it appear as if she had a little bird nest atop her head. The gold-rimmed bifocals perched on the end of her beak of a nose, appeared as if they would fall off at any moment. She would bob her head in a way that reminded one of a robin pulling worms from the earth after a warm spring rain. She spoke in a singsong voice, which became more like a twittering or chirping when she became excited, which was quite often. She always wore dresses that hung down well past her knees, and would have been quite fashionable thirty years before. She had successfully convinced the members of the ACDC that the Boston Strangler was really one of the police officers that had been in charge of the case.

Katie knew that it did not matter if the person was actually convicted at their trial. The only thing that mattered was that you had to convince the members that your theory could have worked. If they could not trip you up or blow your hypothesis, then and only then, would you be admitted into the ACDC.

Next was Harold Simons, who referred to himself as Colonel Simons. None of the residents of Greenbrier could ever prove or disprove that he had held the position of colonel. In fact, they had never really tried. Let him call himself whatever he liked, that was the general feeling in Greenbrier. They all knew that he had probably never served in any official capacity as a colonel, but they still all referred to him as the Colonel.

The colonel sat there with his huge paunch sticking out, as if he had swallowed a barrel of beer, barrel and all. His ruddy complexion and bulbous nose made one immediately think of W.C. Fields. It was a well-known fact that he liked to sit in the Fox and Hound, the local tavern, and regale the patrons with witty tales and theories that he had come up with over the years.

Katie thought that he would probably be one of the easiest to convince. Although within the week, she was sure that he would more than likely make the claim that he had given her the idea of solving the case.

He had been inducted into the club many years before after giving the police his theory about a local man who had been arrested for the murder of his estranged wife. Using his theory, the prosecutors were able to convince the jury of how the murder was pulled off. Of course, the local police had it pretty much figured out from the start, they just could'nt quite prove it. The Colonel had figured out that Jim Green had an accomplice with him the night of his wife's murder. When the Colonel's theories became known, the police had started asking questions that they'd previously not asked. Because of the Colonel,

Jordan Simms was subsequently arrested and implicated in the murder. This was the Colonels claim to fame you could say.

Next on the list of Greenbrier ACDC members was Brenda Cormick. She was short and rather on the pudgy side. Katie's mom would have called her dumpy. Her once mousy-brown hair was now unbecomingly streaked with gray. It reminded one of an old mop that had seen better days. She did not even attempt to cover up the fact that she was getting older, as did all of the other women in the village, by getting a dye job once in awhile. She had always been rather a plain Jane, even when she was young. She was also a spinster; this is where the problem had begun. She and Katie's husband, George, had been something of an item for years, until he looked Katie's way one day and never looked back. Brenda decidedly disliked Katie. That was putting it mildly. You could use the word despised or hated, they were much closer to the feelings Katie believed that she held for her. Whenever George and Katie would cross paths with her, they could see the contempt she held for them cross her face. Katie had heard that Brenda had said that she had drugged George in order to get him to marry her. He would jokingly say that he had been drugged by Katie's beauty, which in fact he had been.

Katie had been a stunning young woman and in fact, she still was. Many of her friends referred to her as gorgeous. Katie was very tall and thin, with chiseled features. Her nose was a bit larger than she would have preferred, but never the less was rather sexy looking her friends told her. Her wide set hazel eyes, which changed colors with her moods, were one of her best features. The color of her hair went anywhere from very blonde in the summer months to auburn in winter. This was not a natural occurrence, but one of choice.

As Katie said, Brenda and she did not like each other. She already knew deep down in her heart that Brenda was going to be her toughest opponent. Brenda would try to trip Katie up no matter what it took. As they used to say, by hook or by crook. Brenda would want to see her fail, and would do her utmost to be the one that made it happen. Even George had forewarned Katie that Brenda would try to thwart her efforts any way she could. Katie would have to be able to convince them as a group that she had the answers to all of the questions that were left unanswered during the trial, namely, how the glove had made it to its final resting place, blocks away from the actual murder scene. It would indeed be a challenge to get Brenda to believe her theory.

Finally, yet importantly, on the list of ACDC members were a couple that had just recently moved to Greenbrier. They were considered new comers to the tiny village, since they had moved there within the last 3 year's. Of course, in Greenbrier the locals considered anyone a new comer who had lived there less than twenty years.

Their names were Tom and Ann Crook. You could search the world over and not be able to find a more suitable name for them, Katie thought. It was common knowledge that they would cheat anyone out of anything. Since their arrival in Greenbrier, they had embittered most of the locals one way or another. When you first met them, they seemed honest enough people. Tom would always make the statement that he was an honorable man. Not many of the locals liked him right from the start because of his arrogance and the fact that he had been in politics in the nearby town of Simmons. Not that anyone had anything against politics or politicians in Greenbrier, they didn't. Nevertheless, it was a well-known fact that he had used his position to, as he said, do favors for those that could return them. He had even been in trouble with the local ethics board on one or two different occasions for attempting to influence a judge.

Ann, on the other hand, came off as such a lady that everyone had been shocked when it became apparent that she was a habitual liar. She also had the reputation of having champagne taste on a beer budget. Not that they did not have money, Katie thought. It was well-known that Tom would sue at the drop of a hat and in most cases, would end up winning. This everyone thought was due to the many favors he had done while he had held the office of supervisor in Simmons. It was said by the majority of the villagers that the Crooks had "all dollars and no sense." He may have money from suing so many people in the past, but he was also known for having very little common sense. This was proven repeatedly in his short tenure in the village.

Katie recalled one instance that stood out in her mind above all the rest. Tom and Ann had been decorating their home when they first arrived in Greenbrier. Ann had told Katie that she had purchased a small nightstand table that had to be assembled. She had later told Katie that the directions had said, "easy twenty-minute assembly."

"Do you know that after three hours he had only gotten it half assembled? Katie, a 6 year old could have put it together faster than that, just by looking at the pictures. He really is rather stupid when it comes to any kind of handy work." The statement had been made in Ann's usual nasty tone. From then on, Ann would hire a neighborhood kid to do odd jobs around the house that needed doing.

It was also well-known that Tom did not like to part with his ill-gotten money, whereas money went through Ann's fingers as if it were water. She would spend exorbitant amounts of money on things that she could have purchased elsewhere for half of the price, and then Tom would refuse to pay for them. He would always state that they had not ordered them, or that the product had been faulty in some way. He would never put the blame on Ann's doorstep, where it rightfully belonged. It was obvious that he never wanted his "perfect little wife" to take the blame.

Tom Crook was a short man, approximately 5'5" tall. His hair was white, with a very prominent cowlick at the crown of his head. His hand would constantly travel to the cowlick as if he were trying to smooth it down into place, which was impossible for him to do. He was rather an ugly little man. He had very close-set eyes, which made one immediately picture a weasel or a rat. His nose was on the large size, which emphasized the smallness of his eyes. His shoulders were extremely small and sloped downward so abruptly from his neck that he appeared not to have any shoulders at all. He always attempted to walk with a gait that made him look like of a man in complete control. This, of course, was a put on; everyone knew who wore the pants in that family.

Ann was an inch or two taller than her husband and so gaunt that she appeared skeletal. She always attempted to hide this by wearing clothing that was much too large for her frame. This had the opposite effect than she had obviously intended, and it did nothing but intensify her gauntness. The extreme pallor of her complexion was testimonial that she rarely, if ever, let the suns rays touch her skin. In Katie's career, she had seen a great number of corpses that looked healthier and in better shape than Ann did.

Even with all of these drawbacks, the first thing that you really noticed about her was her flat face and bulging eyes. When they had first arrived in town, the joke was going around that she looked like a pug dog that had been chasing parked cars and had caught one too many of them. Her lips, which were perpetually drawn down in a frown, gave the impression that she was always angry about something. On the few occasions that Katie had seen her smile, she had noticed that Ann had a horrendous overbite. The overbite reminded Katie of an old mule that should have been put out to pasture long ago. Because of the overbite, her speech at times was rather odd, and when she said any word with an S in it, she made a hissing sound. Katie had also noticed that the right side of her face had a slight droop to it. Katie wondered if perhaps she had suffered from a stroke at some point in her life, prior to coming to Greenbrier. Her hands were long and thin and reminded one of the talons of a predatory bird. They were always adorned with three large diamond and emerald rings that appeared as if they weighed too much for her thin hands to hold. In fact, she wore so much jewelry that Katie thought she might topple over from the sheer weight of it.

Ann also had what most people would say was an obsessive-compulsive disorder. She did not cook because she did not want to have her immaculate kitchen in disarray. Most of the local women claimed that she just didn't know how. Whenever there was a get together that one would have to bring a covered dish to, the locals would avoid her dish like the plague. This happened after some of them had tasted one of her concoctions at The Founder's Day celebration the year of their arrival in Greenbrier.

Terrie, a friend of Katie's, had stopped in the Crook's home soon after their arrival in the village. She said that she could not believe her eyes when she saw Ann cleaning electric outlets with a wet rag. She had warned Ann that it could be potentially hazardous using water near electric. Ann replied, "Well, how do you clean your outlets?" Terrie said that you could see the disgust and revulsion on Ann's face when she had stated that she did not make a practice of cleaning her outlets; she had much more important things to do.

The residents of Greenbrier had also come to find out that Ann was one of the most vindictive and vicious women that had ever drawn breath. Not only did she not have any friends because of her terrible disposition, but it was also a well-known fact that she hated the children and grandchildren that Tom had from a previous marriage. The feelings, they would come to find out, were mutual. The children, two girls, Renee and Sharon, hated their stepmother with a passion. Everything Ann did was for her son and two daughters, and she would exclude Tom's daughters from any family gatherings whenever she could.

She had even gone to the extent of having only three guest bedrooms in the huge Victorian refurbished so that there would be one for each of her three children. While her children would come and stay at their home for the holidays, Tom's daughters would have to stay at the local Inn. Ann said there were not enough spare rooms in the old Victorian. This was ridiculous. The house was so large that it could have easily accommodated his and her children and a number of others as well.

She would also state to anyone that would listen that Tom's daughters would not end up with one red cent of his money. Of course, Tom either did not hear these threats or chose to ignore them to try to keep peace between himself and his wife. Everyone in town knew this woman browbeat him and that he was afraid she would divorce him if he ever opposed her in any way. They were also sure that it was not that he was afraid of losing Ann, but, more to the point, that he would lose so much money if she left him. Years before he had married into a very prominent family in nearby Simmons. When his first wife divorced him, he had ended up with quite a hefty sum of money. His ex-wife's father owned one of the largest businesses in town and had purchased a very expensive home for them when they had gotten married. Upon their divorce, they had sold the home at a very large profit. Ann was often heard to say that she would leave him completely broke if they ever divorced. She had made this statement on quite a few different occasions, and everyone was sure that she would keep her word.

It was not as if Ann were some kind of goody two shoes or anything, Katie thought. It had been rumored that she had had an affair with a postal worker named Denny, the first year they arrived in Greenbrier. It would seem that they had been carrying on with one another for some time, since her car was constantly at the post office. When the word of their affair got back to the postmaster, Denny was moved to a new post office until things cooled down. Of course, Tom ignored these rumors since there really was no way the rumor could be substantiated and he really didn't want to lose the money he had gotten from his first divorce.

These two were going to be very difficult to win over to Katie's side with her theory. They did not like her from the very beginning, and the feelings were mutual.

She was up against a very formable group indeed. Her biggest worry right now though was Brenda. Why did Brenda have to be here tonight? She could have had the decency to be sick or something, Katie thought. Why hadn't she been kept at home for some unexpected reason, for instance by the bubonic plague or some other dreaded disease. No, she knew Katie was trying to get into the club, and she would have crawled through hell to be here to try to keep her from becoming the newest member.

Katie inched her way closer to the podium and introduced herself. This seemed unnecessary. She had been born and raised in Greenbrier and had known everyone in the club all of her life with the exception of the Crooks. Well, she would go by the book. Yes, there was a book. One of the predecessors had written down all of the rules that were to be followed when a new member was trying to gain admittance in to their prestigious club. She would state her case, and then the group would have the opportunity to ask her questions. They could ask anything that they felt would break her theory.

Katie knew she was smart enough to figure this mystery out since she was an avid mystery fan. She had been reading Agatha Christie, Ellery Queen, and Sir Arthur Conan Doyle all of her life. She had watched Colombo, Murder She Wrote, and Diagnoses Murder until she could say the actor's lines before they opened their mouths.

Katie stood before her fellow mystery enthusiasts ready to prove herself. She started to speak, at first with a tremor in her voice. She had never been much of a public speaker, and she was literally terrified. She could feel that all eyes were riveted on her. She could feel Brenda's gaze going straight through her like daggers.

As Katie stood there, she could feel her chest getting tighter with every breath that she took. God don't let me have a heart attack right now she thought. There was not one person in the room capable or, in several cases, willing to save her at this moment.

Mr. Thomson could probably tell the rest of them what to do. At least he would give it his best shot.

Colonel Simons would not have a clue as to what to do, and his enormous girth would more than likely prohibit him from even attempting to help her.

Brenda would let her die where she fell. Of this, Katie was sure. Even though she had attended a CPR class that Katie had held at the hospital, she would feign ignorance as to procedure.

As for the Crooks, it was a well-known fact that they were not good in emergencies. It had traveled around town like a wildfire the day that Mr. Crook had cut down a tree on their property and been pinned beneath one of the branches. Ann had stood out in the front yard screaming her fool head off for help. When one of the neighborhood kids had stopped to ask her what the problem was, she had taken at least five minutes to make known what had occurred. He then asked her if she had called 911, and she had babbled, "I would have, but I don't know the number." By this time, the local police had arrived at the scene. They had heard her horrendous screeching and had assumed that someone was murdering her. When they saw what had happened, they removed the branch from Tom Crook, with apparently little injury to him with the exception of his pride.

Katie decided that Mrs. Finch would be her best bet. As her eyes moved towards Mrs. Finch's frail little body, Katie thought, "She is so frail that she could probably not even perform proper chest compressions, but at least she would try."

"Take nice deep breaths," she told herself. "You can do this."

Katie began to speak again in a quavering voice. "I am going to prove to all of you that I have solved the O. J. Simpson case," she paused gathering her thoughts, "or in any case that I have figured out, at least in my mind, how it could have happened."

Katie was so frightened that her voice did not even sound like herself to her own ears. "Since the murders had occurred so many years ago, I will attempt to reconstruct the events of that fateful night for you. First, I must take you back and remind you of some of the facts of the murder scene."

"A couple had been given a dog by their neighbor, who said that he had found it wondering aimlessly on the street. The couple took the dog to their home. They thought that it had been injured in some way, since it had a great deal of blood on its paws. While at their home, the dog became so agitated that they decided to take it for a walk to see if it could find its way home. The dog ultimately lead them to its home, which turned out to be Nicole's home, and that is when they came upon the grisly murder scene. The police were then summoned to the murder scene, and after conducting an initial investigation, and finding a great deal of evidence including a glove that they believe the murderer had been wearing, they secured the crime scene."

"Some of the lead detectives then went to O.J. Simpson's home on the pretense that they wanted to make sure that O.J. had not been harmed."

"When the police officers arrived at O.J.'s home they attempted to gain admittance to the property by ringing the bell at the gate. When they received no answer after numerous attempts, they decided that something was definitely wrong and that they had to investigate further. Detective Mark Fuhrman, who would become one of the main prosecution witnesses at the trial, jumped over the fence to make sure that everything was all right. He then opened the gate, and the others entered the property. They went towards the house checking out the surroundings on their way. As they searched the grounds for a possible intruder, they encountered O.J.'s large Akita dog, which had free roam of the property."

"After many futile attempts to arouse an occupant in the house, they finally got O.J.'s tenant Kato Kailen to open the door. Kato stated that he thought O.J. had a trip that night and had already departed from the house."

"Kato then went to find O.J.'s daughter, who was staying in a different part of the house. While the rest of the detectives questioned O.J.'s daughter, Detective Fuhrman made the decision to go outside and investigate the property. He later stated that he'd done this to see if there was a murderer stealthily lurking around the property. If you remember, this was hours after the murders had been discovered."

"I've always thought the police would have naturally assumed that had someone been hiding on the property, they would have departed by this time? Everyone figured that O.J. was their one and only suspect at this point, but they needed an excuse to search his property, and this was it."

"Detective Fuhrman said that after he went back outside, with the intention of searching for the murderer of Ron and Nicole or someone who may be there to harm O.J., he made his way along the side of the house. There he noticed a gate leading to a narrow pathway ajar. This, he said, made him want to continue to investigate. As he investigated the path with his flashlight, he claims to have discovered a glove that appeared to be a mate of the one found at the murder scene. I also want you to remember that this glove was in much worse shape than its mate that was found at the murder scene. To the detectives it appeared "moist and sticky and had a gleam or glisten to it." They stated that it almost looked as if it had been dampened at some point."

"What was it doing there? Had the murderer dropped it on this secluded path? That would be the only likely scenario one would think.

"Detective Fuhrman continued down the path where he said he came to an enclosed area, which appeared to be where the gardener potted plants. Here the cobwebs were only broken on the bottom half of the path, not up high where one would expect them to be broken if a man had walked down this path."

"As we all know the glove was the stickler to solving this whole case. It was also the downfall of the prosecution's case, as we would later find out. The defense team attempted to make the jury believe that Mark Fuhrman had gone outside to plant the glove because he was a racist. I believe that if any of the other officers had found the glove where it was originally dropped, the outcome of the trial would have certainly been different."

As she made this statement, Katie, could tell she had everyone's undivided attention. They were definitely interested. This case may have been over for years, but something in human nature made a person want to find the answers to the questions.

"The glove was found directly behind the guest bedroom of Kato Kailen. Kato had stated that while he was on the phone with a friend that evening, he thought there was going to be an earthquake because of loud thumps that came from the back of the house. When further questioned by the police, Kato said that the noise behind his room had been loud enough to startle him quite badly. He said the pounding on the wall had actually made a picture in his room become askew. He then told the officers that he had heard three loud thumps. Later at the trial, he demonstrated what he had heard by banging three times with great force on the witness stand."

"Now as everyone knows there were two prevailing theories in the Simpson Murder case. In my opinion both sides used different pieces of evidence as a magician uses smokescreens and mirrors."

"The defense was sure that Nicole Brown Simpson and Ronald Goldman were murdered by some mysterious person or persons that to this day have not been found. The defense also theorized that Nicole had been murdered because she owed money to someone who had supplied her with drugs. They also believed that Ron was murdered because he just happened to be there." Katie, was shaking so badly just now, that she thought she could hear her knees knocking together.

"I have great difficulty in believing any part of that theory," Mrs. Finch piped up. "When you look at the pictures of Nicole that were shown at the trial, you see a beautiful, healthy 35-year-old woman. There is no way that she appears to have had a drug problem that would have caused her to owe drug dealers enough money for them to murder her. She certainly did not live on skid row or in the ghetto, where people are killed for twenty dollars worth of drugs. Everyone also said that she was such a good mom, who would do anything for her two children. Again, this doesn't sound like someone that is buying drugs from some dealer, who is going to kill her over drug money."

"No it certainly doesn't." Katie said, and continued with her story.

"They also adamantly believed that Mark Fuhrman, one of the detectives on the scene, tried to frame O.J. by planting the glove on his property. They believed this because he had answered domestic calls from Nicole against O.J. in the past. They also believed that he was racially prejudiced."

Katie could see by the expressions on their faces that none of her small audience had put much store in the defense's story.

"Ask yourselves this," Katie said scanning their faces. Why would an experienced police officer attempt to frame someone when he was not sure where that person was at the time of the murders? O.J. was very popular and could have been on national TV at the times of the murders? He could have been out of town, or at some kind of benefit dinner with hundreds of witnesses as to his whereabouts."

"Then again, what if another suspect had been apprehended after Mark Fuhrman had planted the glove as the defense team said he had? Wouldn't Mark Fuhrman have known, since he was the one that discovered the glove, that he would have looked extremely guilty? The detectives would have known immediately that the glove was planted and by whom. Whether you like Mark Fuhrman or not, you certainly can't think that he would have been stupid enough to plant a glove prior to knowing whether O.J. had an alibi." Katie could see that this point had hit home with at least some of the group.

"If you remember at the murder scene there had been fifteen to twenty police officers looking for evidence before Mark Fuhrman arrived at the scene. Could it really be possible that this many trained officers could have missed the second glove in their search of the area had it been there? They had found the left hand glove but not its mate at the scene. In addition, another officer, Officer Riske, accompanied

Detective Fuhrman almost the entire time he was at the murder scene. Could Mark Fuhrman have been stealthy enough to find a piece of evidence that was missed by so many officers? Could he then have hidden it on his person on the way to O.J.'s house so that he could frame a man that he did not even personally know?"

"I believe that then and there the defense's theory about Mark Fuhrman planting the glove should have been deemed illogical by people with any intelligence at all. After all, at that very moment, Kato could not be positive as to the time when O.J. had departed from his home. At this point, the exact time of the murders had yet to be substantiated. It should have been obvious that unless Detective Fuhrman knew for sure the exact timeline, he wouldn't have attempted to frame O.J. with the glove, since it later could have been found that O.J. had left the property prior to the murders."

"Now, if Mark Fuhrman had wanted to frame O.J., as the defense said. He could have very easily dropped the glove in the yard on the way to the front door, since he was walking behind the other officers as they made their way onto the property. On the other hand, he could have just as easily dropped it when he jumped the fence to allow the other officers admittance to the property. After all, after he had jumped over the fence for a very short time he was alone on the property. One would think that he would have dropped it in the yard to have it discovered immediately, instead of carrying it around with him to find such a secluded spot to place it."

"Well, he wouldn't have dropped it until he knew for sure that OJ was at home that night." This statement came from the Colonel.

"But he never did find out any exact times from Kato. If you remember, Kato was very unclear as to the time that OJ had left his property," Mrs. Finch piped up in her twittering little voice. "Now please allow Katie Scarlett to continue with her story."

"We can also pretty much discount the defense's theory that it was someone that hasn't been discovered, even after all of these years. As Mrs. Finch pointed out, Nicole certainly did not appear to be the type of person that someone would kill for no better reason than the defense thought that she might owe them money for drugs. On the other hand, if someone had wanted to kill Ron Goldman, they certainly would not have waited until he was at Nicole's house to do so. They would have attacked him before he entered Nicole's property so there would not be any witnesses." Katie was attempting to get her thoughts in order.

As she glanced at the upturned faces in front of her, she prayed that she could make them understand her theory. Mr. Thomson and Mrs. Finch were listening intently to her story. Katie knew that they were making mental notes as to questions they could later ask her. Colonel Simons sat there trying to reposition his huge girth in his chair with very little success. Tom Crook's hand was attempting to smooth the cowlick into place, while his wife Ann sat staring at her bony fingers, apparently trying to make sure that none of the prongs on her rings had become loose. Brenda glared at her, making Katie feel for all the world like a first grader asked to speak in front of the entire class.

"The defense was continually attempting to muddy the waters in this case, and apparently did a good enough job since they got their client off," the Colonel said.

"I really don't think that the defense team expected to do this because of their reactions at the trial when the verdict was read." Katie replied.

"If you remember, F. Lee Baily gave a fleeting look of disbelief that was gone almost before you could notice it. Having been a top-notch trial lawyer for so long, he hid his reaction well. "

"Johnnie Cochran cocked his head as if he weren't quite sure of what he had heard. The look of confusion that crossed his face was quickly replaced with a triumphant smile."

"Then we have Barry Sheck, another defense team lawyer. He had an utter look of disbelief on his face as the verdict was read. He looked completely confused as if there had been some kind of mistake made. His reaction spoke volumes to everyone watching. I truly believe that he was in shock over the innocent verdict he had heard."

"After the police had done a thorough investigation of what they referred to as "both crime scenes," they then came up with their own theory as to how the glove had gotten to this secluded pathway behind Kato's room. They believe that after O.J. committed these two horrendous crimes, he drove the Bronco home and haphazardly parked it out in front of his gate. Then according to the police, O.J. walked around his fence through his neighbors' yards and jumped the high fence banging into the back of Kato's room as he did so. They believe this is what made the thumping noise Kato later claimed had sounded like an earthquake was about to happen. The police and the prosecution then surmised that when O.J. landed on the other side of the fence, he got down on all fours to crawl down the path, and while doing so he inadvertently dropped the bloody glove on his own property where it was later discovered."

She paused to let this sink in, hoping that her voice would sound less nervous than it had been.

"O.J. then apparently stood up, according to the police, and entered his house so that he could get cleaned up before leaving on his trip that night. The limo driver had testified that he saw a six-foot-tall, well built African American enter the house while he was waiting to take O.J. to the airport."

"I believe that the prosecution story is a bit more accurate than that of the defense, with the obvious exception of O.J. jumping over the fence, dropping the glove as he did so."

"As we all know, no one has ever been convicted of the brutal, senseless murders. I believe the reason for this is that there has never been anyone else on the prosecution suspect list, because they have always known that they had the correct person right from the start. They were so sure that O.J. had committed the murders they never attempted to look for anyone else. The case could never be solved since the prosecution has always said that O.J. had dropped the glove where it was found, and the defense, that it was the police. When in fact I know that it was neither of the two."

All eyes were riveted on her. The tightness in her chest had begun to subside, even though her hands continued to tremor. Tom Crook was still attempting to smooth the cowlick down, while Mrs. Finch sat there bobbing her head in rhythm to Katie's words.

"I would like you to ask yourselves this question: If O.J. had committed these murders, as the prosecution asserted why would he have to jump over a fence to get onto his own property? When they later checked the fence where they believe he'd gained admittance, they said that the vegetation, which was very thick on the high fence, was undisturbed. How could a man of O.J.'s stature have accomplished this? One would naturally assume that if any size person had climbed over a fence that was covered with plant growth, that there would be evidence of it. The answer could be that they had to have a reason for finding the glove where it was. It would also provide a reason for the noise that startled Kato that night. They could not say that O.J. had entered through the front gate, since there would have been no reason for him to take the glove to the narrow pathway and drop it. There also would not have been any reason for the banging sound that Kato had heard. I believe that if O.J. were trying to hide the glove, he would have found a much better place to do so than on his own property. He would also have been very careful not to draw attention to the hiding place by banging on the wall of an occupied room."

Katie went on as everyone sat listening. Their eyes were all glued on her face, and she began to chew on her bottom lip.

Katie again filled her lungs with a great breath of air before continuing. "I want to tell you how I believe the glove came to be found behind O.J.'s house on that fateful night. This, as you all know, was the biggest obstacle for the prosecution. If they could have without a doubt proven that O.J. was the only person that could have dropped the glove on his own property, then it goes without saying that he also had to be the murderer of Nicole and Ron."

Katie's head felt as if it were going to burst from the pressure she was under at that moment. They were all looking at her, different expressions crossing their faces. Most of them were concentrating intently on her story, with the exception of Ann Crook, who sat there with a look of complete bafflement on her gaunt face.

"I had other questions during the trial that puzzled me. If you remember, they found O.J.'s Ford Bronco parked in a haphazard fashion out on the street by the front gate. Why was it out on the street and not in the drive where he usually parked? If indeed, he had parked his vehicle out there in plain view, why would he then take the chance of encountering someone outside of his property, by walking around the entire fence to find a convenient place to jump over. After all this man was one of the most recognizable football players of all times. He had won the prestigious Heisman trophy. Even with my limited interest in football, I could have readily recognized him if I had encountered him somewhere. If indeed he were the murderer, would he have taken the chance of being seen by neighbors or anyone else that could have identified him by walking around the outside of the fence. In all probability, he would have known that if someone had seen him, they would have reported it to the police after the murders had been discovered. This has never made any sense to me; when he could have very easily entered his yard via the front gate without any suspicion."

"It had struck me as peculiar right from the beginning why O.J. picked that night to park his Bronco on the street instead of driving in through the gate as he usually did. Perhaps he did not want to alert the inhabitants of the house that he was entering the property. If he had driven onto the property, the lights from his vehicle, or the sound of the engine, could have alerted someone inside of his presence there. If they had heard a vehicle drive up, they may have come to the door to see who it was. If O.J. had just committed this double homicide, it would make sense that he would be covered in blood. It may not have been noticeable if he were wearing dark clothing, but he certainly would not want to bring attention to the fact that he had left the property around the time of the murders and then returned later. He would have been smart enough to know that even though the murders had been committed blocks away, eventually the police would come to his house to question everyone there. People remember when something odd happens during a homicide investigation. On the other hand, if the witnesses stated that they thought he was at the property during the time of the murders, it would have taken some of the suspicion away from him." She was getting braver as her story progressed.

"There is something else that has always been stuck in the dark recesses of my brain. Having been a nurse for many years, I've always wondered if O.J. could have even accomplished this. He played football for years and had so many knee injuries during his career that one would assume that it would be next to impossible for him to accomplish this feat. The defense team had stated that his knees were so bad that he had to use a golf cart instead of walking the course while playing golf. From the beginning, jumping over the fence, and then getting down and crawling around his own property had sounded, to say the least, odd."

Katie was breathing a bit more easily now.

"I would also like to ask you this question. If it had been a stranger prowling around outside of the house, wouldn't O.J.'s dog have alerted the occupants? One would expect it to. I know when someone enters my yard; my Lab, Sam, puts up a terrible fuss." As Katie's gaze went to her neighbor Mrs. Finch, she could see her head bobbing in agreement to this statement.

"The dog had not attempted to stop the police when they came through the gate, since more than likely it was accustomed to people, such as deliverymen and gardeners entering that way. On the other hand, if someone were sneaking in from a different direction, namely, the back path of the house, you would think that the dog would have alerted the inhabitants, especially, one would think, if there were banging on the walls as there had been that night. I would think that the dog would have barked to let the inhabitants know that someone was trespassing, wouldn't you?"

"We are all intelligent enough to know that the murders had been planned in advance, since the murderer had a knife with him." Katie thought to herself that at least most of them were intelligent enough. "This really can't be disputed by anyone." Katie looked in Brenda's direction as she said this.

"What if O.J. had been planning on killing his ex-wife as the prosecution believed? He would have dressed in dark clothing to camouflage himself in the darkness. What was the likelihood that the murderer, if it were someone other than O.J., had a black knitted cap just like the one O.J. had worn in a movie that he had been in, and at the trial it was disclosed had his hair on it? Or that the murderer had a pair of Bruno Magli shoes, which were size twelve. The same size and type that O.J. wore. A very limited number of these shoes, in that size sold in the entire country. Remember, they were very expensive shoes, which the average person probably would not have purchased. If you stop and think about it, what is the likelihood that the killer also had a pair of Aris Light size XL gloves, identical to the ones that O.J. had worn on a national TV broadcast? Moreover, it was later found out that Nicole had purchased that exact same gloves at Bloomingdale's for O.J. in 1990. He had also been seen wearing the gloves at different times from 1990, to 1994 when the murders were committed."

"Coincidences in a murder trial do happen, but there have always been too many coincidences in this case for my liking," Katie said.

Again, she scanned the upturned faces before her. She did not believe that anyone could dispute the evidence that had been discovered during the police investigation.

"Now, take yourselves to the night of the murders. If O.J. had planned to kill his ex-wife, as the prosecutors in the case had surmised and I believe. He could have gone to her house and somehow enticed her to come to the door. We will never know why she went outside that night. She was waiting for Ron Goldman to come to the house, so perhaps she thought that it was him at the door."

"It was later stated that she had been planning on taking a bath because the bathtub was full of water. Something had made her stop what she was doing and go to the door that fateful night. When she came to the door, O.J. could have easily overpowered her. He was a large man who had played football for years. He also had to his advantage the surprise of attack. In all likelihood, she would have been unprepared for an attack on her person. After overpowering her and taking her life, O.J. is surprised by the arrival of Ron Goldman. O.J. more than likely had not planned on a double homicide, but he would have to get rid of this eyewitness. If you remember, Ron was returning a pair of glasses that Nicole's mother had left at the Mezzaluna restaurant where he worked. O.J. would have had no choice in this matter since Ron would definitely be able to identify him."

Katie once again stopped to take a great breath of air in before she continued with her narrative. She was praying that this torture would soon be over.

"After committing the murders O.J. could have left Nicole's property through the rear entrance so that he would not encounter anyone that may recognize him. The police had found bloody shoeprints leaving the premises in that direction. The shoeprints matched a pair of shoes owned by O.J. There were also blood drops to the left hand side of these shoeprints, which DNA tests later proved matched O.J.'s blood type. It was later in the investigation that the police discovered O.J. had cut his left middle finger. Could this be another coincidence? I doubt it. I believe that O.J. then got into his Bronco and drove the short distance home, leaving the Bronco parked on the road out front, as I've stated, so he wouldn't draw attention to himself from the people staying with him."

Katie gave a momentary pause and tried to gather her thoughts.

"Up to this point of my story, I believe that the prosecution had come up with a very likely scenario of what had occurred that night. It is after this point that I believe the prosecution and my scenario begin to differ. I also believe that my theory is much more likely than theirs had been." She stated this with much more confidence than she actually felt.

"I will tell you what I think actually occurred that fateful night. What if after O.J. committed these murders he then entered his property as one would expect him to, through the front gate. He would have been carrying with him the bloody glove, the knife, and various other bloody items that he had to dispose of. Could it be that O.J. inadvertently dropped the bloody glove upon entering his property? After just committing a double homicide and having to catch a plane in a very short time, he would be in an extreme hurry to get into his house to get cleaned up. In all probability, he would not have even noticed that he had dropped the glove upon entering the gate. But, how did the glove get from where he had dropped it to where it was later found? I believe that I have found the answer to this question."

Katie searched for the words that would make her theory plausible. "We can dispute most of the prosecution's theories about how he entered his property very easily. As I previously stated, how could O.J., have jumped over the fence without disturbing the vegetation that was growing on it? The most agile gymnast would more than likely not have been able to accomplish this feat. So how could a man of O.J.'s size, with bad knees to boot, have done this? How did he then manage to crawl down the path on his hands and knees and not disturb the path in some way? This was not a well-traveled path, if you recall the photos presented at the hearing. It was overgrown with vines from the fence, and had a great deal of leaves and twigs scattered on it. One would assume that the officers would have noted any disturbance to the path."

"It would have been impossible," Mrs. Finch, stated more to herself than the group.

"That is why I believe that the prosecutions theory is flawed."

Ann broke in before Katie could continue. "So far, all that you have proven is that O.J. probably didn't drop the glove where it was found, and that the police more than likely didn't place it there either. Did the glove grow wings and fly back to where it was found?" Ann asked with a sneer, which made her overbite even more prominent. "Or perhaps it grew a pair of little legs and walked to the place where it was discovered?" She hissed the words through tightly clenched lips in her usual snippy tone.

"No, I don't believe the glove grew wings. Anyone with the least bit of common sense would know that," Katie said in an equally snippy tone. "I believe that there were legs involved," she went on. "No, before you ask, the glove didn't grow them," she said pointedly looking from Ann to Brenda. "I also don't believe it was a pair of legs that carried the glove to where it was found, I believe that it was two pair of legs." Everyone appeared puzzled at this.

Katie continued with the story after the rude interruption by Ann.

"Now consider how the trial would have gone if the glove was never found at O.J.'s residence? The glove was the thing that both sides attempted to use in their favor. If the glove had not been found at Rockingham, it would have made it much easier on the prosecution to prove O.J.'s guilt. After all the prosecution had a mountain of evidence against O.J. at the actual murder scene. Finding the glove on his property had made it appear that the police may have been trying to frame him," she looked at her audience and then went on.

"If you get rid of the second glove completely, I believe that O.J. would have been found guilty of the murders of Ron and Nicole. After all, they had Nicole and Ron's blood on the Bronco. They also had Nicole's blood on a sock found on his bedroom floor. Her blood on the steering wheel of O.J.'s Bronco should have sent red flags up, one would think."

"The defense always stated that Nicole's blood could have been found on O.J.'s property for one reason or another. They said that since they were still on friendly terms after the divorce, she could have had a superficial wound that could have explained it being there. However," Katie said, "there was absolutely no reason for them finding Ron's blood on any of O.J.'s effects."

"The prosecution also had the size twelve shoeprints from the expensive shoes that O.J. owned. They also had fibers and hair samples that matched O.J.'s at the murder scene. All of this evidence in itself more than likely would have been sufficient to prove O.J. guilty."

Katie stood there sorting through her mind for her next words. She wanted to make it as simple as possible.

"Think for a moment of what would have happened had the glove been found at O.J.'s residence as soon as the detectives entered the yard. It would be very unlikely if all of the officers had found the glove that they would all have been in on trying to frame O.J. for the murders. If this would have happened, again I believe that O.J. would have been found guilty." She paused for just a moment before continuing.

"I believe that the glove was what locked the prosecution's case up completely. I also believe that I have found the key to unlock this puzzle."

They sat there looking at her, different expressions on all of their upturned faces. Brenda still had the sneer on her face that she had from the beginning of Katie's story. Ann was looking at the ceiling, and it was impossible for Katie to know what she was thinking. The rest of the group was giving her their undivided attention.

"I am absolutely sure that the glove had been dropped by O.J. when he entered the front gate of his home," Katie said. "Of this fact I am positive. I also believe that except for an occurrence that happened completely by chance, it would have been found in the front yard exactly where he had dropped it."

Her audience looked stunned. Even Ann seemed to perk up at this statement.

"We all know that the glove was found on the secluded pathway," Mr. Thomson interrupted Katie's story, his dentures clicking as he spoke. "How did it get from the front yard where you believe it was dropped to the path, Katie? Was it by supernatural means, did the glove levitate to the area? We are all rather intelligent people, so we can discount any supernatural interventions, I would think."

"No, there was nothing supernatural about it," Katie said pointedly. "I truly believe that this is the perfect example of everyone, "not seeing the forest for the trees." Everyone thinks that this was one of the most difficult cases ever. I, on the other hand, think that it was simplicity itself," Katie said with great confidence.

"We have all seen dozens of pictures of what the police called the second crime scene, which was O.J.'s house. There were the officers in charge of the investigation, Kato Kailen, and O.J.'s daughter present. As far as any of us know, there were no other human beings present that night."

Katie could tell that they were searching their minds, trying to remember exactly who had been there that night.

"It amazes me that no one else has come up with the same theory that I have. We all watched the case on TV. We saw all of the major role players repeatedly, until almost all of us could identify every one of them on sight. However, I believe it was just like in the movies where we all tend to pay attention to the well-known movie stars and usually give very little thought to the bit players. The bit players, as you all know, are the ones that we see, but their importance just doesn't grab our attention until it is pointed out to us." You could have heard a pin drop in the quiet room.

"You probably haven't realized it, but you have all seen the culprit that placed the glove where it was found in the narrow pathway over and over again. As a matter of fact, both the prosecution and the defense showed pictures of the culprit many times. They both mentioned the presence of this bit role player so many times that I can't believe someone other than me hasn't found the truth."

"Now wait a minute, Katie, you have said that two pair of legs transported the glove back to where it was found," Mr. Thomson said. "You certainly don't think that two of the detectives plotted to frame O.J. It would be very difficult to believe that one had done this, let alone that two officers would do such a thing. On the other hand, it would be even more difficult to think that Kato and O.J.'s daughter carried it back there. I mean you said that we have all seen the culprit, and since the only ones there when the police arrived at O.J.'s house were people who have all been pretty much eliminated from the suspect list, are you trying to tell us that someone that no one knows about was trying to frame O.J.? That would just bolster the defense theory."

"No," Mrs. Finch piped up. "You are wrong, Mr. Thomson. Katie Scarlett said that we have all repeatedly seen who dropped the glove where it was ultimately found. So it couldn't have been some anonymous person attempting to frame O.J."

"I'm pretty doggone sure that the one that dropped the glove where it was discovered hasn't got a clue to the meaning of the word frame, Mr. Thomson. I believe that the word does not even exist in his vocabulary. As a matter of fact, I think that the culprit was this man's best friend, since his moving the glove from where O.J. originally dropped it to where it was ultimately found, eventually got O.J. acquitted," Katie said.

"Wait a minute, Katie, this is getting rather confusing. You said that O.J.'s best friend moved the glove from where he dropped it back to the path. I don't recall any of O.J.'s friends being at his house that night, except for Kato, who really can't be considered a best friend." This statement came from the Colonel.

"That's right; I don't believe that Kato would have been a close enough friend for O.J. to trust to do this for him, if O.J. had told him to remove it, which he did not. Of this, I am certain. I also think that out of all of the witnesses, Kato was probably one of the most honest," she said this as she scanned their faces.

"Well, Katie Scarlett, you must mean that it was his daughter or one of the police officers in the case. Do you think that Mark Fuhrman found the glove where you think O.J. dropped it, and for some reason known only to him, he moved it back to the path?" Mrs. Finch looked doubtful about this.

"No, I truly believe that Mark Fuhrman found the glove exactly where he said that he did, and that he never touched it. I actually believe that every word Mark Fuhrman spoke was the absolute truth, especially the part about where he found the right hand glove on that fateful night."

They all gave her doubtful looks as she finished this last statement. Katie was quite sure that the defense team had pretty much done its job in convincing everyone that Mark Fuhrman was a rouge cop. She knew that the man may have many faults, but as far as his testimony about the glove, she believed he had been telling the absolute truth, and she was going to prove it.

"I got it," Tom Crook said. "You think that after O.J. left his property, he knew that he had dropped the glove, and he called this friend and had him go to his house and move the glove."

Mrs. Finch was shaking her head. "No, if O.J. had called someone and told them to get rid of this piece of evidence, this person would have completely removed it from the property. He certainly wouldn't have just moved it to the back pathway so that it would later be discovered by the police."

"Did O.J. call someone and have them move the glove? You would think that the police would have found out about the call if one had been made," Ann insisted.

"No, there was no call made." Katie waited just a moment before continuing. "Even if O.J. could have called the one that moved the glove to where it was found, which was an impossibility, there would have been no way for O.J. to make him understand what he wanted him to do. This particular friend has an extremely limited knowledge of the English language."

They all looked at her as if she had just dropped down from Mars.

Katie went on. "The friend moved the glove because he wanted to, not because O.J. told him to."

They all appeared stumped by this statement.

"Now you're trying to tell us the friend just happened along and moved the glove, and that the friend speaks a totally different language from O.J.," the Colonel said, attempting to rearrange his great girth to a more comfortable position.

"I can't remember anyone at O.J.'s house speaking a language other than English. I'm sure that I would remember if there had been a foreigner present," Mr. Thomson said. As he was fluent in seven different languages, there was little doubt of this, Katie thought.

"The friend isn't a foreigner at all," Katie said. "He more than likely was born right here in the good old USA. I'm just saying that he speaks his own language that is impossible to translate."

Katie could see when it began to dawn on Mrs. Finch. Her head began to bob up and down almost in a rhythm. She then began to twitter and chirp. "We all have been so stupid, haven't we? It really was this man's best friend, wasn't it, Katie Scarlett?"

"Whatever are you going on about, Mrs. Finch?" exclaimed the Colonel.

"We have all been trying so desperately to find the person that dropped the glove where it was discovered. What if it wasn't a person at all?" Mrs. Finch's eyes were almost popping out of her head as she said this.

Katie smiled at Mrs. Finch. "By God, I think you've got it," she said.

"God's name should not even be mentioned," Brenda glared at Katie. "This was a terrible tragedy that God would never have condoned."

"No, he certainly wouldn't have," Katie said. "But I do believe that there is something having to do with God's name that can solve this mystery."

They all sat there looking at her as if she had lost her mind with the exception of Mrs. Finch, who Katie believed knew exactly what she was talking about.

Brenda said, "You really shouldn't use the name of God in any way, shape or form during this story. It's almost blasphemy to do so."

"I'm not really using the name God, but I do have to use a shape or form of it to tell you who put the glove where it was found."

They all continued to stare at her. Brenda looking very disgusted indeed. The rest of them asked her what she meant.

"If you ask yourselves what the anagram of God is, you will find the identity of who dropped the glove where it was found. Once you have accomplished this you will also have the answer to this mystery."

It took the majority of them only a few moments to register this. Katie thought that most of them had indeed been shown the truth by what she had said. She could see by the expressions that crossed their faces that the light was beginning to dawn on the majority of them.

Mr. Thomson, having been a schoolteacher was one of the first to figure it out. You could almost see the light bulb go off above his head.

Mrs. Finch, who Katie believed had already come to the correct conclusion, said in awe, "It has been right under our noses the entire time, and none of us saw it with the exception of Katie Scarlett." Katie had known that Mrs. Finch would be one of the first to work it out.

Ann and Tom sat there with completely blank looks on their faces. Ann said, "What is an anagram for God's sake?"

Mr. Thomson gave her a rather pitying look. "An anagram is a word or phrase formed by reordering the letters to form another word or phrase. " Ann continued to give him a blank stare. He went on, "For instance when you take the word *tap*, and you change the letters around, you end up with the word *pat*."

Ann was just not going to get it; Katie knew this when she said, "I don't remember any Pat in the Simpson case."

"Think of what the anagram for God is, Ann. If you rearrange the letters in the word God what do you come up with?" The blank look remained on her face. "The word God spelled backwards is dog."

There was complete silence from the group while they waited for this to sink into Ann's head.

Mr. Thomson said, "Ann, it was the dog. That is why Katie said two pairs of legs and man's best friend."

"I can't believe it. The dog carried the glove to the path?" Tom Crook looked amazed.

"I will tell you what I believe happened that night," Katie said as she gathered her thoughts.

"Keep in mind that O.J.'s dog had the freedom to meander about the premises, because the yard was completely fenced in. Everyone had mentioned that there was a dog present at O.J.'s home that night, including the prosecution and the defense teams. Unfortunately, they just never gave it much more than a passing thought. Remember the dog was a bit player in the midst of all of the celebrities."

"I know that some of you have had dogs at one time or another," Katie continued. Dogs have an extremely keen sense of smell, which is thousands of times greater than that of us humans. What would be the first thing the dog would do picking up the scent of fresh blood?" Katie gave them a questioning look. "Just as their wild ancestors have done for thousands of years, I believe the dog would have picked up on this scent immediately, and he would have picked the glove up and taken it to a secret location where he could chew on it in solitude. As any dog owner knows, not only would he chew on it, but he would also more than likely shake it vigorously. If you have never owned a dog, you more than likely have seen TV programs in which a dog, or one of his undomesticated relatives, has done just this when it has found something to chew on."

Katie was very confident in her story by this time. She again scanned the faces of her audience. They all were giving her their full attention at this point, even her adversary Brenda.

"I, along with many others, had at first believed that O.J. had indeed been framed by the police. No one wanted to believe that this Heisman trophy winner and, as the defense called him, "National Icon" could be capable of such a horrendous crime. That was up until one evening when an unexpected occurrence happened that changed my entire outlook of the case." Katie had a look of complete control at this moment.

"It just so happened that one night while George was out playing cards with some friends, the truth became apparent to me. I had been lying on the couch while watching a TV program, and had, as was common for me, fallen asleep. I was startled awake from this sound sleep by a thunderous thumping on my front door. The pounding on the door was so loud, that I thought someone was attempting to break it down. When I looked out the window of the top of the door, I did not see anyone. The noise continued for a long time, and I finally mustered up the courage to go and investigate where the noise was coming from. I armed myself with a .22 caliber pistil and edged my way to the door." Katie paused for a moment. The people in the room who knew her could tell by her face that she had indeed been scared that night.

"As I eased my way to the door, believe me when I say by this time my heart was pounding nearly out of my chest, I peeked through the window at the top of the door. I couldn't see anyone, but when I glanced down towards the porch, I was shocked to see what was happening. My dog, Sam, a female Lab, had found something that she was vigorously shaking. In fact, she was shaking it with such a vengeance that her large body and head were striking the door repeatedly, and I thought she was going to injure herself. As I went out to investigate, feeling less threatened by this time, I discovered exactly what was happening. Sam had found a blood-smeared glove that George had been wearing while out hunting that day. She was shaking the bloody glove so furiously that her mammoth head and body kept hitting the bottom of the door. This had been what produced this thunderous noise that had startled me from a sound sleep."

It was as if everyone in the room suddenly became frozen solid. In all of Katie's life, she had never been the center of such attention as she now found herself.

She went on knowing that they were all holding their breath to hear what she had to say.

"Talk about serendipity. What was the likelihood that I would have been startled awake, out of a sound sleep, just as the banging on his room had startled Kato? It had just so happened that it had been hunting season for deer, and George had bagged a very nice buck. He had processed the deer in the garage, and as George usually did, he had left the mess for me to clean up. George had left several rags and a pair of gloves with deer blood smeared on them on the floor of the garage. Sam had found one of them before I had had the opportunity to clean up the garage and decided that it was too irresistible to just let it lie there. She had brought the glove to the front porch, where I discovered her with it after the horrendous noise had awakened me."

She definitely had their attention now. They were hanging on every word.

"So, now we have how I believe the glove could have been transported to the back path of the house. The dog having detected the smell of blood, had found the glove where O.J. had dropped it on entering his property, and as any dog would do carried it off to a secluded area."

The looks they were giving her left little doubt that they believed every word she was saying.

"We now also know why the webs were only broken on the bottom half of the path leaving the top ones unscathed. The huge dog would have only broken the bottom three feet of cobwebs as it was transporting the glove to this secluded area. It wasn't O.J. crawling down the path that had done this, but the huge dog walking down the path that broke the cobwebs in this way."

"This would also explain what the great banging sound heard by Kato was. It was not O.J. banging on the side of the house after jumping over the fence. It was the dog, doing what a dog would naturally do, shaking and playing with this newfound toy. All the while, the dog would not be paying any attention to the fact that its body was thumping into the side of the building. This large of a dog confined in such a small area would have made a noise that would have aroused the dead. After all, my dog had awoken me on the night that I spoke about, and I am the soundest sleeper in the world. The sound of the dog banging on the outside of Kato's room that night would have sounded like someone pounding on the outside of the house. Or in Kato's words like an earthquake was going to happen."

Katie could see the transformation as it occurred. The nonbelievers were now believers.

"I had another question while reaching my conclusion. Did they do any DNA tests on the glove to see if it had dog saliva present on the material? They had tested for blood, hair and other fibers, but they had never said if they checked for dog saliva. If they had, I believe that they would have found it. Why else would the glove have appeared to still be moist and sticky, with a gleam or glisten to it, after all of these hours? The answer could be that the dog had gone back on several occasions to chew on the glove, and its saliva had kept it moist and sticky."

The Colonel looked awe struck as he made this next statement. "That's why the police didn't see any human footprints or other signs of a disturbance back on the path. There were none to be seen."

"That's right. They had asked Mark Fuhrman if he had noticed any footprints from a human on the secluded path, and he had said he had not. Could he have noticed if a dog had walked down this path? It would be very doubtful. He also stated that the path was very dirty with leaves and twigs along it. This is exactly the kind of place that a dog would take something that he wanted to hide so that he could chew on it later at his leisure."

"My God, that's why the glove looked so different from its mate. It appeared that the fingers were stuck together and that it was all wrinkled up," Mr. Thomson said, almost in a whisper.

"Yes. The saliva along with the blood on the glove would have made it very sticky. This would have made parts of it adhere to one another as the dog chewed on it," Katie said with a smile.

As she stood there, her small, but now attentive, audience, having taken in the entirety of what she had said, had many different reactions cross their upturned faces. Old man Thomson had the look of great respect across his face. He had been her teacher and he had always said that she was one of his best biology students. Katie had not thought that he would believe her capable of coming up with a satisfactory conclusion to a murder that had never been solved.

Mrs. Finch had started to bob her head halfway through Katie's narrative. By the time she finished, Katie thought that it was going to fall right off in front of all of them. At any moment, it appeared as if she would produce a huge egg as she twittered and bobbed her head, cackling like an old hen the entire time. Katie heard her murmur, "I knew that someone would solve this case sooner or later, but I never thought that it would be our own Katie Scarlett."

Colonel Simons gave a great laugh. "I knew that it was something just like that. I just never bothered to tell anyone because I knew that sooner or later someone would want to use this to get into the ACDC, and I didn't want to ruin anyone's chances." As he said this, he looked all the world like a giant toad that had just eaten a huge bug and enjoyed every bite of it. Katie had known that eventually he would try to take the credit for her theory. She had thought he would at least wait until the whole process was over before doing so.

The Crooks sat there obviously trying to come up with a question that would break Katie's theory. Tom began to try to smooth the cowlick into place and then stated that he did not think that it was a very good idea to try to hang this murder on O.J., since he would in all probability attempt to sue her. This would be something that a person who has sued numerous people would say, Katie thought.

Katie explained the double jeopardy law to him. She told him that O.J. could not be tried again, since he had been found innocent of the charges already. In addition, he had placed himself in a position as a public figure, so you could say just about anything that you wanted and he could not sue you over it, as long as it was just an assumption.

Mr. Thomson, giving her a look of admiration, said, "I truly think that if they would have heard your account of what had happened, during the trial, things would have turned out much differently than they did." This was a great compliment from someone as intelligent as Mr. Thomson and Katie knew immediately that at least he believed in her theory.

Ann had been looking at her bony hands that were adorned with the beautiful diamond rings. She raised her eyes to Katie's and said, "I have never heard of anything as ridiculous as a dog picking up a blood-soaked glove and shaking it hard enough to wake the inhabitants inside a house."

This coming from a person who had openly stated that she had never, nor would she ever, own a filthy dog was ridiculous. Moreover, she had no idea of their behaviors. Everyone knew that she hated animals and would call the local police if one ever dared to step on her property. Since most of her neighbors owned animals, she had made a total nuisance out of herself by doing this. The police had become so tired of the numerous calls that they had been heard saying she had better be being murdered if she wanted them to answer any more of her calls. They also made a point of saying they would take their good old time in getting there the next time she called.

Now Katie looked toward her greatest adversary, Brenda. Brenda sat there haughtily looking at Katie as if she could kill her. This was one of the most foolish things that she had ever heard, Brenda said. Katie knew that in all probability, she believed her story, but this would not stop her from attempting to keep her from getting in to the ACDC. Katie could tell from the look on her face that she was going to question her strenuously just to try to ruin her chances.

Brenda cleared her throat and said. "I still believe that the glove was planted there by the police. What makes you think that it had not been and that the dog did it?"

Katie answered her question with one. "Again, how would the detectives on the case know that O.J. was even at home on this night? He could have had an airtight alibi for all that they knew. Why would they have taken the chance of removing a piece of evidence and taking it to his house the night of the murders? Another thing is that there had been at least fifteen police officers at the murder scene. None of them had seen the second glove. If you remember Mark Fuhrman had arrived after they had searched the property for evidence."

She then asked, "If O.J. had dropped the glove why didn't he pick it up immediately?"

You could tell by Katie's voice that she was getting angry. "Perhaps he didn't realize he had dropped it until he found it missing when he went to his room to get cleaned up for his trip. Perhaps the dog ran off with it so quickly that he didn't have the chance to get it away from him. Everyone that has ever owned a dog knows that a dog takes great pleasure in a game of fetch. Usually the more that you attempt to get the ball back, the more enjoyment the dog has in keeping it from you. The only thing different in this game was the dog had the glove instead of a ball. I still believe that is the reason O.J. had to come up with the story that he was out chipping golf balls that night. He would not have known if someone had seen him while he was searching the yard for the glove after he had discovered he had dropped it. He had to make up the story about the golf balls, in case someone had seen him searching for the glove in his yard and informed the police of what they saw. What better excuse could he have come up with for looking around his yard in the middle of the night, than he was looking for golf balls?"

Brenda sat there not knowing what to do next. She thought that she had the upper hand, but Katie knew that she had convinced all of the others, even the Crooks, and that Brenda stood alone with her doubts.

She then said, "I seem to remember that Kato said he and O.J. had gone out in the yard when Kato had heard the noise or shortly after. Where was the dog with the glove then?"

Katie looked her square in the eye this time and said, "He had probably already taken it behind the house and dropped it there. You never having owned a dog," Katie pointed out, "probably have no idea of how they act. Any dog, whether it is a poodle or a St. Bernard, will do the same exact thing when they find something that they want to play with. They will grab it and shake it vigorously. They will throw it in the air and then chase it as if they are playing catch by themselves. Not paying attention to where they are going, they often run into furniture and the like. As I told you before that was what made the noise back behind Kato's room. The dog took the glove back to the small enclosure and while playing with it, his body repeatedly hit the side of the building, making the horrendous noise that Kato had heard. He would have come out if he heard O.J. and Kato talking, but he would have left the glove in its safe hiding spot in the secluded path."

Katie went on. "Who would even notice the dog except O.J., and he definitely wasn't mentioning it? None of the people involved in the case paid much attention to the fact that he was present. As I said, we have all seen numerous pictures of the crime scene and the dog, but no one noticed it because of the great hubbub about O.J. being guilty or innocent."

"I have often wondered what would have happened if the dog had been standing in the yard with the glove in its mouth when the police arrived at the house." Katie said. "They would have immediately known what had happened. As I always said, murderers do sometimes get lucky, and I believe that this occurrence was O.J.'s bit of luck. His dog really was man's best friend in this instance. My bit of luck was that Good Old George did not clean up after himself after processing the deer he had gotten. If he had, and Sam hadn't found the glove with the deer blood on it, I, in all probability, wouldn't have ever figured out what I believe happened that night." This seemed to take the wind out of Brenda's sails, at least temporarily.

Mr. Thomson was sitting there with a very odd look on his face. "I can't believe it. Everyone in the case had mentioned the dog so many times. I just can't believe that they never thought of your theory, Katie. By God, now that you have told us what actually occurred that night, it really does become quite apparent. If the police and the prosecution would not have concocted such an elaborate theory, it may have been clear to everyone right from the start what actually happened."

Katie smiled. "Well, they had to have a reason for the glove being found where it was and for the cobwebs being broken down near the ground like they were. They also had to have a reason for the noise that Kato heard. They just didn't have any other explanation, so they came up with the one that they did to explain everything."

"You would think that the police would have thought of your theory about the dog," the Colonel interjected.

"It has always astounded me that since almost every large police precinct in the country have canine units someone hasn't come up with the same theory as I have," she said a little embarrassed.

"I mean they use the canine units to track missing people. A bloodhound will stay on a trail for miles because of the scent the victim leaves, even if there is no blood present. They also use cadaver dogs to find dead bodies with such accuracy that it sometimes astounds us humans that anything can have that much greater a sense of smell than we do. They quite often use dogs at investigations to show which way a criminal left just by using their keen sense of smell. Perhaps none of the detectives owned a dog and they didn't know that the scent of blood has such an overpowering attraction to them. I truly believe that if a canine unit would have been called into O.J.'s property on that night, the case would have been solved very quickly indeed. One of the dogs on the unit would have gone directly back to the path and found the glove. I also believe that the outcome would have been quite different than it was."

Katie then asked if anyone else had any questions. No one seemed to be able to come up with anything that could trip her up. There were one or two questions, but other than that, everyone with the exception of Brenda and, perhaps, the Crooks seemed satisfied with her theory.

Katie was then asked to leave the room. This she knew was so that they could discuss her theory and then take a vote on whether she would be the newest member of the ACDC. She knew that only one person would strenuously oppose her becoming a member and that would be Brenda. She would be taking an awful big chance if she did this out of spite. The ACDC would not tolerate its members keeping someone out just because they disliked a person. They would not keep someone from being a member because of vindictiveness or, in the case of Brenda, hatred.

Katie excused herself and went to sit in the great room. As she gazed around the great room, she thought to herself, at least you have some accomplishments, Katie."

The ACDC had taken over the mansion three years ago to have a permanent meeting place in which to conduct their meetings. They had commissioned her to paint this very room, since she had a small side business doing faux painting. Her business had started out by her painting the pediatric ward at the hospital free. She had painted murals on the walls to make the pediatric unit less hospital-like for her little patients. As word of her talent spread, others wanting to make their homes and businesses different from the norm sought her out. Katie now had to turn jobs down because there just were not enough hours in the day. George had told her many times that she should give up nursing and make the painting a full-time job, but she could never give up a career that she truly loved, even though they were so under paid and overworked at the hospital.

Katie had painted the great room a very vibrant red, then sponged an extremely dark red overtop of it. She had finished the walls with a gold filigree stenciling. The ceiling, which she had painted with cream and golden clouds, gave the appearance that one was standing outside looking up at the heavens. It had turned out to be one of her most impressive works thus far, and she was quite proud of it.

Her thoughts now went back to why she was here. Her stomach was in knots. She had for so long wanted to be in the ACDC that she did not know what she would do if they turned her down. As she sat there, she tried to take her mind off the fact that she would be humiliated if she did not get to be in this prestigious club. She also knew that she would never live it down in the little village. News whether she had made it or not would spread like a wildfire through town within a day or so. The two gossip centers to first receive the news would be the local beauty salon, The Curl Up and Dye, and the local watering hole, the Fox and Hound. She and George often went to supper or to imbibe in a couple of pints of beer at the latter. She frequented these two establishments, and she would be mortified if she had to face the patrons defeated. Katie might still be able to go to the Fox and Hound because Good Old George would be with her to bolster her courage. However, she knew that she would never be able to face the girls at The Curl Up and Dye. She would feel like such a failure.

Another gossip center was Dixie's Diner. Katie knew that she would have to go without eating one of Dixie's fantastic meals for quite sometime if she did not make it into the club.

After what seemed a lifetime, the huge double mahogany doors to the library opened, and Katie rejoined the group. She tried with all of her might to swallow the huge lump in her throat, but she could not get it to go past her Adam's apple.

Katie looked at the group and could read in their faces that she had come out the victor. Mrs. Finch had a huge smile on her wrinkled little upturned face. She had always liked Katie since Katie had taken care of her elderly husband in the hospital before his death. After Mr. Finch's death, Katie had looked in on her to make sure she was taking care of herself, especially since she was an insulin-dependant diabetic and did not always eat properly. Katie would take her homemade soups and fresh vegetables from her garden. They would then sit on the front porch swing and talk about how the world was changing so much everywhere else except here in Greenbrier, where nothing much ever happened. At least this had been the case up until the next couple of weeks, as they would soon learn.

Katie's former teacher, Mr. Thomson, whose face she could never read, had the slightest upturn to the corners of his mouth. Ever since she had been his pupil in high school, she had a great fear of him, which over the years had turned to respect. She also always had the greatest respect for his profound knowledge.

Colonel Simons sat there; his great girth looking for all the world like the chair that he was occupying could not hold his weight for more than a few more seconds before it shattered into kindling. He had a huge smile on his face. As Katie knew, he more than likely was already in the process of coming up with a story of how he had given her the idea to solving this mystery.

Tom and Ann Crook had a look of total indifference on their faces. Katie was sure they would make the point that, even though they were here in Greenbrier for such a short time, they had already gotten into the club; before she did. Katie had always wondered whether they had bought their way into the club; they certainly did not seem intelligent enough to get in on their own. It was difficult to believe that they could have solved a mystery on their own without the help of at least one member of the club. Did she feel this way because, like most of the other residents of Greenbrier, she did not like them, or was she totally underestimating their abilities?

Now her eyes went towards Brenda. If looks could kill, she would be six feet under. Brenda stared at Katie for what seemed an eternity and Katie returned her stare. She thought that Brenda was going to cry when Mr. Thomson announced that Katie Scarlett Adams was the newest member of the ACDC.

The quiet room then was filled with the buzz of voices. Congratulations were given to her, some with great and honest warmth; some, much cooler. Brenda got up from her armchair and excused herself, saying that she had to leave. As the room emptied out, Katie could hear her reprimanding the Crooks for not standing with her on keeping Katie out of the club.

As Katie made her way home that night, she felt such a great amount of pride that she could have burst at the seams. She had come through the greatest challenge of her self-proclaimed mystery career with flying colors. Katie was walking on air as only this kind of triumph could make one feel. If she could only have seen what the future would bring, she more than likely would not have been so light-hearted.

The next day as Katie entered The Curl Up and Dye for her weekly hair appointment, the gang greeted her with many congratulations. She knew that Mrs. Finch must have been the one to tell them about her success at being voted into the ACDC. If Brenda had had a hair appointment, which Katie was sure she did not, she would have cut out her own tongue before she would have given Katie any kind of credit for her achievement.

Ann would also not be one to tell anyone of Katie's accomplishment. She truly believed that she and that husband of hers, were the only ones worth giving any credit to.

When she was leaving the beauty shop, she caught a glimpse of Joni, who owned The Curl Up and Dye, gliding towards her. That was the only way to describe her walk. She was a tall, voluptuous redhead, with legs, as the men would say, that went from her perfectly rounded derriere all the way to the floor.

She always dressed in clothing that accentuated her curves, even though this was not necessary, since in all probability she would have looked just as good in a burlap sack, Katie thought. Whenever she entered a room, all heads would turn to watch her. The men just could not help themselves, and the woman wanted to discover the secret of her walk. Katie had overheard one man say at a party that he could be content for the rest of his life just watching her walk towards him.

Her most stunning features in Katie's opinion, were her emerald green eyes. When she turned them towards you, she seemed to gaze into the very depths of your soul.

Her complexion was as flawless as the finest porcelain and the envy of every woman in the village. Not one fine line could be detected on her lovely face, and for this reason, no one could determine her actual age. When asked, Joni would jokingly say that she was somewhere between the ages of consent and senility.

She did have the quick temper that is associated with redheads, and a flash from her emerald green eyes could stop you in your tracks. This was not a rare occurrence. Katie had witnessed it many times in the years that she had known Joni. She was one of the kindest and most gentle woman that you would ever want to meet, once you became her friend. However, there were certain behaviors that she could not stand. She especially disliked people who did not have any common sense or who failed to use it if they did have any.

As she glided towards Katie, her French bulldog puppy, Fiona, was closely following her. Joni had just gotten her, and the puppy had become her constant companion, obediently following Joni everywhere she went.

The little round bundle of fur was blissfully playing with her favorite toy, a stuffed spider monkey. She would toss the monkey high up in the air, and then catch it in her tiny mouth as it landed. Her droopy little jowls, with there loose flesh, would sway as she pounced on the toy. The puppy reminded Katie of Alfred Hitchcock because of the loose folds of skin that surrounded the pup's tiny mouth. They would jiggle and shake as she ferociously shook her prey in the mock game of kill the monkey, the whole time not seeming to notice that her tiny body was banging into Joni's long, shapely legs.

Fiona's pink jewel-studded collars, flashed in the bright lights of the salon, as if it were encrusted with real diamonds instead of paste ones.

As the two-approached Katie, Joni flashed her incredibly perfect smile at her. "I hear that congratulations are in order for you getting into the ACDC," she said. "I knew that you could do it." Her voice was almost like a purr. She gave Katie a hug and Katie detected the fragrance of her expensive French perfume. "I think it is just wonderful that I have a friend with the intellect to be in the club. You know I think you are just about one of the cleverest people I have ever met, Katie, especially in solving mysteries." Her green eyes were searching Katie's face as she said these next words. "I wonder if there were ever a murder in Greenbrier, you could figure it out?" This statement would come back to haunt Katie in a very short time.

Several days after her acceptance into the club, Katie received a phone call. Mrs. Finch was all-atwitter. "Katie Scarlett, you are never going to believe what that horrible Mrs. Crook has done." Katie could tell by her voice that she was beside herself. "Baby, went over to that cruel woman's house and she came out with a broom and hit him with it." Mrs. Finch was so indignant about this that you would have thought that Ann had walloped her with the broom instead of Baby.

"I just don't know what to do," she twittered on. "If any harm ever comes to Baby I will know who is responsible, and I will make her pay for it."

This Katie could picture Mrs. Finch doing. She had never had any children, so Baby was exactly that. He was her baby and her constant companion ever since Mr. Finch had passed away fourteen years before.

"She told me that I had better keep him out of her yard because she sets poison out for the wild animals and that he might get into it." Mrs. Finch was becoming increasingly angry.

"Oh, Katie Scarlett, I just don't know what I would do if she brought harm to my little fellow," her voice trembling as she spoke. After about fifteen minutes, Katie had finally succeeded in getting Mrs. Finch calmed down. Mrs. Finch thanked her, and they hung up.

Katie told Good Old George the story when he arrived home from work that afternoon. He could not believe that anyone would be heartless enough to get Mrs. Finch that upset, with all of her health problems.

"I told you they were going to be nothing but trouble right from the start, didn't I, Katie? I don't know which of them is worse: him, having been the supervisor of a dinky little town like Simmons, or her acting all ladylike until her true colors show, and you find out what a real bitch she is."

"Perhaps we better warn Joe." Joe was their local police chief and a friend of George and hers for many years. "You better call and tell him that these people are putting poison out that a child could happen upon," Katie said.

As George made the call to Joe, Katie started supper. She could hear him in the distance telling Joe what had happened with Mrs. Finch. When he was done with the call, George came to the kitchen and told her what Joe had said.

"Joe told me that he has had more complaints about the Crooks since they moved here, than he has had over the previous three years, about all of the other residents combined. Can you imagine being hated that much? It would bother anyone else, but I think they thrive on it."

As they sat down to a wonderful feast of grilled chicken breasts, creamy potato salad, stuffed mushrooms and her famous apple pie, they never would have foreseen what trouble these people were actually going to bring to the little village. As it turned out, it was trouble enough to disrupt the lives of almost the entire community.

Two days later Katie received another call from Mrs. Finch. She was more upset than Katie had ever heard her before. Baby was very sick; he was trembling and could not keep his food down. She asked Katie if she could come over and look at him. Not that Katie was a vet or anything, but she had owned dogs all her life and would frequently get calls from people who had pets and could not get them to the vet's immediately. The local vet, Doc. Weaver, was ready to retire and unfortunately did not have anyone to cover for him when he and his wife went out of town, which they frequently did.

Katie went over to Mrs. Finch's house and examined Baby. He was definitely very ill and could barely raise his head. His heartbeat was so erratic that she thought he was going to die before they could get him to the vet's office in neighboring Simmons. His little black and white body shook uncontrollably as they placed him in his little doggy bed so that he would be as comfortable as possible on the way to the vets.

The vet examined him thoroughly and when he was done asked, "Has this dog been exposed to any kind of poison in or around your home?"

"I would never have anything that Baby could get into out in the open. I am very careful about that," Mrs. Finch told him.

The vet wanted to keep Baby for observation for a couple of days. It was the longest trip that Katie had ever made from Simmons back to Greenbrier in her life. It was only ten miles, but it seemed to take forever for them to get back home.

Mrs. Finch continuously muttered, "I know that woman poisoned him, she said that she would and she did, Katie Scarlett. How could anyone be so cruel as to hurt my poor little Baby?" Katie's heart went out to her. Baby was the only thing that really mattered to this poor old woman, and if he died, it would more than likely kill her.

Two days after the trip to the vet's, they received the dismal news. Katie was with Mrs. Finch when she received the phone call. She had never witnessed such devastation on anyone's face before in her life. Baby would not be coming home. He was too old to fight anymore and he had passed away in the night.

Mrs. Finch's first words were, "I am going to kill that woman."

Katie knew without asking that she was referring to Ann Crook.

The vet had confirmed that indeed, it had been poison that had taken the little dog's life. He thought that antifreeze was what had killed poor little Baby. As Katie tried desperately to comfort Mrs. Finch, her thoughts were going a million miles a minute. If that horrible woman killed Baby she would kill her herself, Katie thought. She did not have any proof that Ann had done this cruel thing, but on the other hand, there was not a doubt in her mind that she was capable of doing it.

Mrs. Finch sat on her couch trembling. Her shoulders were heaving with each breath that she took. Her small face had tears streaming down the crevasse that crisscrossed its wrinkled little contours. The tears, which followed the creases down her face, dripped from her tiny chin unnoticed by her. Katie was trying desperately not to cry, but she could feel the tears as their warmth made paths down her face.

Katie sat with her for hours. She listened as Mrs. Finch reminisced about how she and her husband had gone to the dog pound, and had found Baby as a puppy. He had been a little black and white ball of fur she said. The man that had worked at the shelter had told them that he would be put to sleep if no one adopted him, so they had taken him home with them. He was one of the greatest joys of their lives. Katie herself remembered this adorable little dog running around the yard, his squeaky little bark at times had a way of annoying her, but she would do anything to hear that little bark right now. She would also like to be able to take the great pain away from this poor frail little woman whose heart was breaking in front of her very eyes.

After making sure that Mrs. Finch was going to be okay, Katie went home and told George what had happened.

"That woman is going to go too far some day." The expression on Georges face showed that he loathed the woman.

"How much further could she go than killing a defenseless little dog like Baby?" Katie asked, tears streaming down her face. "I never knew anyone who would hurt an animal in such a way as she has done."

"We can't even be positive that she is the one that did it, Katie."

"You know as well as I do that it was her. She told Mrs. Finch that she put poison out, and there isn't a doubt in my mind that either she or that wimpy husband of hers killed that poor woman's dog."

"The dog could have found the antifreeze somewhere else you know." She could tell that George did not really believe this by the expression on his face.

"Baby never left the yard until that woman started to entice him over to her yard." Katie was wiping the tears from her eyes. "Mrs. Finch said that she had caught her giving him treats to get him to come over to her yard. Then she would call the police and tell them that Mrs. Finch deliberately let him come over so that Baby could do his business in her yard instead of in her own. I have never met anyone that enjoys stirring up trouble the way she does."

"She really is a horrible, vindictive bitch," George muttered. He rarely cursed, but under the circumstances, Katie could not really blame him.

It was the second week in November and the weather had changed drastically and more quickly than she had ever before seen. Where it had been in the sixties a day or so ago, it had now dropped off into the thirties. The first snow flurries had turned into inches of accumulated snow, and everyone in Greenbrier realized that winter had officially arrived, no matter what the calendar said.

Katie was awakened one morning by the insistent ringing of the telephone, and her African Gray parrot, Pepper.

Whenever the telephone rang, Pepper would whistle, scream, talk, and make a total nuisance of himself. This went on throughout every conversation. Katie believed that he did this because he thought that she was speaking to him, since he could not see anyone else. On the other hand, it could be that he just did not want to be left out of the conversation.

As Katie made her way to the telephone, she was not overjoyed at being awakened on her only day off this week. She tried to focus her eyes, which were getting worse by the day. It was Terrie calling from the hospital. Terrie was a wonderful nurse and they had become quite close working together over the last fifteen years. Katie was hoping that nothing had happened that she would be called in to work. She was worn out from being so short staffed and picking up overtime. Terrie's voice was quite excited, which was unusual for her, since she usually had nerves of steel in any kind of situation.

"Katie, have you heard?"

"Heard what?" Katie asked in a yawning voice.

"Ann Crook is dead."

"Terrie, everyone knows that," Katie said in a sleepy voice.

"You mean that you have already heard?" Terrie sounded shocked.

"Well, yes, after all I was the one that solved her murder at the Halloween party." Her brain was still foggy having just woken up.

"No. I'm not talking about the Halloween mystery you solved," Terrie said in an ominous voice.

Terrie went on even more excited than before.

"Ann Crook really is dead. They brought her body into the morgue last night."

Katie was stunned. "What happened?" she asked not the least bit tired now. The haze had lifted immediately with the words she'd heard. It was as if someone had thrown a bucket of ice water on her.

"They say that she drowned in her hot tub, but they have to wait on the autopsy report before they can verify it," Terrie said.

"Do you know any details yet?" Katie knew she should not be nib nosing, but for some reason she felt that she had to find out exactly what had happened.

"No, I don't know what could have happened. I was talking to the ambulance driver, you know, Ted; he was the one who brought her body in, and he said that the gas meter reader had found her. He really didn't know any other details, but he did tell me that the police were investigating."

"Listen," Terrie said, "I will keep you up to date from this end. How about running down to The Curl Up and Dye and seeing what you can find out, okay?"

"I'll try my best," Katie told her.

She tried to reach Good Old George on his cell phone, but he must have been out of the tower range. There was no use calling anyone else; she knew they'd all be at Dixie's Diner or the beauty shop. It was much too early for any one to be hanging out at the Fox and Hound, with the exception of the Colonel and Dick Carlson, the local drunk.

Katie figured she would try her luck at the diner. She was hungry anyway, and Dixie did serve one of the best breakfasts you could find anywhere.

Katie got on her bike and peddled down to the diner.

As she pulled up in front of the diner, she knew she was not the first person to have heard the news. The parking lot was full to overflowing. Everyone was coming but no one was leaving. She should have known, that this being such spectacular news in the small village, that everyone would want to know exactly what had happened.

As Katie was trying to find a table, she heard her name being called. She knew who it was, even in this crowd. Not many people used both her first and middle name, but Mrs. Finch always used both.

"Katie Scarlett, come over here, dear." As Katie approached her table, she was greeted with a huge smile from Mrs. Finch. She had rarely seen Mrs. Finch in such an animated mood. Katie could tell by the expression on her face that she was nearly gushing.

"Did you hear about that wicked woman finally getting what she deserved, dear?" Katie thought that this was a bit cold, even though everyone did dislike the woman. She told her that she had heard and asked her if she knew any details.

"They found her dead in her hot tub," Mrs. Finch stated with great satisfaction. "I don't know what happened, and I really don't care, as long as that woman is gone," she said with true feeling.

They could pick up bits and pieces of conversation from the surrounding tables. The most prominent voice that could be heard was that of Colonel Simons.

"I knew that someone would do her in before too long," he said in his deep baritone voice. "No one ever liked that woman, and I can see where her husband was filled to the gills with her demands."

Katie was thinking to herself that he really should not be accusing someone of murder before the autopsy report was in. No one could even be sure what had caused her death yet. He went on in an even louder voice than before. "She has hurt so many people in this village that it is about time that she meet her maker and paid for her sins," he said as he took a great gulp of coffee, which nearly made him choke.

Everyone knew that Ann and Tom had cheated the Colonel out of a vast amount of money. When they had first moved to town, Ann had wanted to furnish the old Victorian in period pieces, and she had wheedled her way into the Colonel's good graces. She had one of her cronies from Simmons, an antique dealer, appraise the furniture that the Colonel was selling to her for a great deal less than the actual value. It turned out that he didn't get a fraction of the actual worth of the furnishings. She then went around bragging to anyone who would listen that she had "taken the old goat for the ride of his life." They had all felt very badly about this since they were sure that the Colonel was on a very fixed income. They all knew that he would never have considered getting rid of the family heirlooms unless he was quite desperate for the money.

As she sat there, she felt a pair of eyes drilling through the back of her head. Katie did not even have to turn around to confirm that the owner of the eyes was Brenda Cormick.

She could hear some of the conversation that Brenda was engaged in even at this distance.

"You do know that Ann and Tom cheated George Adams out of a great deal of money, and it cost him a great deal in attorney fees to try and recoup it, don't you? It also cost George business from the people of Simmons, since the Crooks told everyone they had been ripped off by George."

Katie could not believe what she was hearing. She knew that Brenda hated George and her, but to stoop to this level of low was almost impossible to believe.

The recipient of her words, who Katie could not identify without turning around said, "Well, Brenda, the Crooks ripped everyone off, including you, I've heard."

There was dead silence from the table for several moments before Brenda replied with a great deal of anger in her voice.

"Whatever are you talking about?"

The voice went on in a rather smug tone. "I heard you were going to buy the old Victorian that they purchased, and we know for a fact that they stole it right out from under you. You were going to make it into a B&B from what we hear, and when the deal was almost complete, the Crooks came in with a higher offer and your deal was spoiled."

"I wasn't serious about starting a B&B. I had just thought that it would give me something to do," Brenda stated with no conviction at all.

Everyone knew that Brenda needed money. She had been living off her inheritance from her parents for as long as any one could remember, and the money had to be running out. She had planned to sell her house and move into the B&B so that she could live out the remainder of her life with at least some income, and would not have to go into the nursing home located on the outskirts of town.

"You have to admit there are many people who wanted her dead," Brenda said.

It amazed Katie that everyone seemed to have come to the same conclusion. They all thought that Ann had been murdered instead of having died accidentally. The woman, as Katie knew, had absolutely no common sense, so she may have succumbed out of sheer ignorance. Knowing her, she could have been cleaning light fixtures while standing in her hot tub. Nothing would surprise Katie at this point.

Her attention was abruptly brought back to Mrs. Finch, as she stated the same thing that Katie was thinking. "You know it could have been an accident," she said with a smile. "I have seen Ann cleaning her goldfish pond in the rain without unplugging any of the pumps or lights. Perhaps we are all jumping to conclusions just because she was so hated."

Hated was not the word for it. From what Katie could hear of the conversations that were going on around them, hate was not quite a strong enough word. It wouldn't have surprised Katie in the least if at any moment the whole group burst out in a chorus of "Ding Dong the Witch is Dead", from the movie "The Wizard of Oz."

Katie excused herself from any further conversation by saying she had to go home and do some work, and left the diner. She really didn't have anything pressing to do, but she wanted to think about what had happened on her own.

As Katie biked home, her mind was so full of everything that she had heard that she almost went into the path of an oncoming car. Katie was lucky that the driver was paying attention and swerved into the other lane. She could see the driver's mouth going ninety miles a minute, and could guess that she was being called some rather vulgar names at the moment.

At home, Katie tried once again to get hold of Good Old George. This time she was successful. After she had relayed the news, including all of the gossip down at Dixie's, there was complete silence on the other end of the line.

"George, did you hear what I said?"

There was a moment more of silence, before he said, "This is going to cause trouble in our village just because of the gossip." There was a vast degree of foreboding in his voice. "I will try and get hold of Joe when I get home and maybe we can nip this in the bud before the whole town runs rampant with gossip."

Katie hated to tell him, but it was a bit late for that. She told George that she loved him and they hung up.

That night the local chief of police came to their house. Joe and George had been friends for as long as anyone could remember. Joe was one of the most handsome men you could imagine. He was tall and dark, and could have been a double for Richard Gere in days gone by. He commanded attention wherever he went because of the Clint Eastwood like way he had about him. He never had to say much, his manner spoke louder than words, just like Dirty Harry. Everyone that knew Joe liked and trusted him. Katie was happy that he was their friend and not an enemy.

He was also Greenbrier's most eligible bachelor. There was not an unmarried woman, or for that matter, a few married ones, in Greenbrier who had not set her cap for Joe in the past, to no avail. He had been desperately in love with his high school sweetheart, and they were planning to get married as soon as they graduated. This never came about. Joe's "angel", as he called her, died in a terrible automobile accident on graduation night. Her death had killed something in Joe. He would date different woman now and then, but he said he could never take the chance of falling in love again.

George offered Joe a cold beer, which Joe gladly accepted. He was not on duty, so he could kick back with his old friend and relax for a while.

"I guess that you've already heard the hubbub going around town," he said in his easygoing manner.

George confirmed this with a smile.

"The way gossip runs rampant in this town, I would have been shocked if you hadn't heard by now," Joe said.

"Do you know that everyone is on the suspect list, even me?" George said as he sat down in the chair across from Joe.

"I have heard just about everyone's name in town mentioned so far," Joe replied.

They sat there in silence, each taking long swallows of their cold beer. The two of them were just like a couple that had been married for years; they were just happy to be together and really didn't have to speak to communicate their thoughts.

They would sometimes go fishing for hours on a Saturday afternoon. When George returned from one of their outings, Katie would ask what they had talked about. George would say, "We really didn't talk about that much," which was in all probability true. They had been friends for so long that they could almost read each other's mind.

"It's going to be at least a week before the autopsy report comes in," Joe said, taking another sip of beer. I am going to treat this as if it were a suspicious death to be on the safe side." They all knew Joe did not want to write it off as an accident just in case it was murder.

He didn't want the reputation that he had messed up the only big case to have come his way in their little village. He had been a deputy when the only murder in Greenbrier had taken place, and it was nearly bungled, because the chief at the time had put it down as an accident.

"We have to keep the locals from jumping to the wrong conclusions," Joe said.

"Otherwise we are going to have a free for all, with everyone blaming everybody else. If we lived in the city, no one would even know that his or her neighbor had died. Here in Greenbrier you can't visit someone without everybody knowing about it."

This was true. Katie was quite certain that the minute Joe left they would get at least five phone calls about his visit.

"I can't give you any details just yet, but I can tell you that Mrs. Crook's body was found floating in her hot tub. The coroner could not give even a close time of death because the body was in such hot water. The only thing that I am sure of is that she was seen last night between eight and nine o'clock by no less than six people." He took another long hall from the icy beer. "She was out in her yard and had yelled at several of the neighborhood kids as they walked home from scouts. The parents had gone over to ask her why she'd done this, and she said that they had walked through her flower beds, which of course the boys denied doing." You could read in Joe's face that he and more than likely the parents did not believe Ann's version at all.

When Katie looked over at George, she could tell he was thinking the same thing.

After a bit more conversation, Joe stood up and said his goodbyes. Katie could tell from the many years of knowing him that he was much more troubled than he was letting on.

Katie went to bed early that night since she was scheduled to work the next day. George said that he was going to stay up and watch some television for a while. She kissed him goodnight, as she had for the last twenty-some odd years, and went up to bed.

George had call after call that night. Some people would start out on the pretense of needing his advice on some building or other and then mention that they had seen Joe's car parked in front of their house. Others would come right out and ask what Joe had been doing there. Oh, small town life, one just had to love it.

Things calmed down somewhat over the next four days. Rumors still circulated, but everyone was getting back to their own lives.

On the fifth day after Ann's death, Joe once again was a visitor in their home. Without any preamble, he said. "Ann Crook was murdered." They sat there in stunned silence. Their worst fears realized.

"How?" was the only thing that George and Katie could say.

"She was poisoned," Joe replied. "If it wasn't for the autopsy we would have never found it. They found wine spiked with antifreeze in her stomach contents. There was a small amount of food in the stomach, but they are sure that the wine contained the antifreeze. The wine wouldn't have hidden the taste of the antifreeze, so the coroner is baffled as to why Ann would have drank it," Joe sighed as he said this, a worried look crossing his face. "Even if the taste could have been hidden by the wine, the wine would have a rather thick consistency that Ann surely would have become aware of while drinking it."

Katie's thoughts flew to Mrs. Finch. What had she said? She would kill Ann if she ever found out that she had poisoned her little dog, Baby. Katie had even questioned her at the time to see if there were any poisons that Baby could have gotten into on her property. She had said there was none. When Katie had questioned her about anything being in the garage, she said that she did not think so, but they had gone to have a look anyway. Katie had thought that perhaps antifreeze was leaking on the floor from Mr. Finch's old car, which had been parked there ever since his death. This theory was soon dispelled as she looked in the garage and saw his old VW Bug. Even with her limited knowledge of cars, she knew that the old VW Bugs do not have a radiator, so there could not be any antifreeze on the floor for Baby to ingest. Katie had forgotten that they owned a Volkswagen, not having seen it in so long.

They had always been such a sight, the little old couple puttering along the narrow streets on their way to church Sunday morning. They always parked in "their parking place," which no one else would have thought of parking in. After church, they would go off on a Sunday afternoon drive through the countryside to pick berries or just for the ride.

Katie was so ashamed of her thoughts about poor little Mrs. Finch. She had been in such declining health since the death of her little dog that Katie had to stop in on a daily basis on her way from work just to check up on her. Mrs. Finch had not been checking her blood sugars as frequently as she should and her diet was very poor indeed. On the other hand, she had made a remarkable comeback, Katie thought, since they had first heard about Ann Crook's death. It did make Katie wonder.

She was thinking that George and Joe might be having the same thoughts. After all, she had told them what had happened and everything that had transpired from the first time that Ann had hit Baby with the broom.

Katie was startled back to reality by George's voice saying, "By God, I'm glad it's you and not me investigating this mess, Joe. With so many possible suspects, it's like putting your finger in a beehive and trying to figure out which bee stung you."

After Joe departed, Katie took the phone from the hook. She knew it would be the same as the last time, when after Joe's last visit, the phone had rung repeatedly. She did not want to answer questions about why he had been there. In fact, Joe had asked them to keep this under their hats until he found out what was going on in the DA's office. She certainly did not want to lose his trust.

The next evening Katie was out back by the fishponds preparing the ponds for the long dormant season. She had been so busy in the fall that she had neglected doing this until now. Her attention was drawn to her perfectly manicured hedgerow, now bare of their beautiful green foliage. As she watched, she saw what appeared to be a white bird nest making its way across the top of the thick hedges. Katie could not see anymore than this, but she was sure it was Mrs. Finch making her way along the other side.

The little nest was moving along at a steady pace, and soon Mrs. Finch appeared at Katie's rear gate.

"Katie Scarlett, have you heard the news?" Mrs. Finch asked in her singsong voice. Katie noticed that her voice was no longer as frail as it had been in the previous weeks.

"What news is that, Mrs. Finch?"

"That terrible woman was poisoned," she stated with so much satisfaction in her voice that Katie was shocked.

"Where did you hear this?" She knew that local gossip moved quickly, but this was ridiculous.

"Oh, it's all over town, dear. Everyone knows about it," she stated matter-of-factly.

"I also heard that they have taken Tom Crook in for questioning." This statement was made in such a triumphant manner that Katie thought Mrs. Finch was almost gloating.

Katie had been expecting this of course. The husband was always the prime suspect when a wife died. Especially under such circumstances as these.

Katie told her that she had not heard about this. This was true. Joe had not mentioned this last evening.

"You would think that the chief of police being so close to you and George would have told you when he was over last night," she said with a knowing little smile.

"We really aren't privy to what Joe is doing on the case." Katie knew this sounded like a false statement even to her own ears.

"If he is arrested, it will be like killing two birds with one stone, you know," she said with a little wink. "You know, Katie, he is hated almost as much as that wife of his had been."

Katie did not want to go into too much detail at this point. She had promised Joe that she would not, so she had to watch every word she said.

Katie asked Mrs. Finch if she wanted to go down to Dixie's for a cup of coffee and she readily agreed.

She noticed as they walked that Mrs. Finch's gait was much steadier than it had been. She probably noticed this because of her profession. Nurses often noticed a person's gait.

"You seem to be feeling much better, Mrs. Finch."

"Oh, yes, indeed I am," she said. "I feel as if the weight of the world has been lifted from my shoulders since that terrible woman died. It could also be because my mind is so consumed with this mystery that I just can't seem to think of anything else, including my aches and pains."

They entered Dixie's Diner and made their way to a corner booth.

Dixie herself came to wait on them. The first words out of her mouth were, "Did you hear the news? They have taken Tom Crook in to question him."

"Yes, we heard," Mrs. Finch, said. "Isn't it just what we all expected?" She gave Dixie a knowing look.

As they ordered their coffee, Katie looked around. Old man Thomson caught her eye. He motioned for her to come to his table, and she obediently went.

"As you know we are going to be holding an ACDC meeting on Tuesday night," he said eyeing her up. "Will you be able to attend?"

Katie told him that she would, and he asked her to remind everyone that belonged to the club to join them at the regular time and place. As if you could keep anyone away, Katie thought. Everyone knew what the major discussion would be about, and she instinctively knew that everyone would be present.

"I don't think that Tom Crook will be there," he said with a sly little smile. "Not if Joe is doing his job properly, one would think."

"Do you think that he is going to be arrested?"

"It would only make sense, Katie; he is our best suspect at this point."

She told him that she would let everyone know about the meeting and returned to her table. Mrs. Finch and Katie sat there savoring the rich coffee that Dixie had brought to them. As they sipped the delicious brew, she reminded Mrs. Finch about the meeting on Tuesday. Mrs. Finch twittered that she would not miss it for the world.

"After all, if we all put our heads together, we should come up with the correct answer to this puzzle, don't you think, dear? Especially with you being in the club and being such close friends with the lead investigator." Mrs. Finch was peering over the top of her bifocals as she made this statement.

"I shouldn't really discuss anything that Joe tells us, Mrs. Finch. After all it is only conjecture at this point."

"Nonsense, Katie Scarlett, Joe is one of your best friends, and I am sure he is telling you much more than you are letting on."

After they had finished their coffee, they returned to Katie's house. As they parted company, Mrs. Finch said. "You will tell us all you know, won't you, Katie Scarlett? "You know you being in so tight with the chief of police and all," her little wrinkled face was beaming as she said this.

"Joe really doesn't take us into his confidence as much as everyone seems to think, Mrs. Finch. After all you were the one that told me about Tom being taken in for questioning."

"Nonsense, dear. I am quite sure that you know a great deal more about the case than you are telling me." With this, she turned on her heel and made her departure, head bobbing as if she were closer to eighteen than eighty.

Katie told George all about her afternoon when he arrived home that night.

"Remember, sweetheart, don't tell them that Joe has been to visit or they will hound you for every bit of information he's given us."

"George, everyone already knows Joe has been to the house again, so they already suspect us to be well-informed of all the details."

"Just don't give them too much information okay." As he said this, he took her in to his arms and gave her a playful kiss.

How could she keep what Joe had told them to herself, she wondered. He'd said that Tom was no longer the prime suspect in the murder investigation. He had called George that very afternoon with the new information. Joe had said that after questioning Tom on his whereabouts the day of the murder, Tom had what appeared to be an unshakeable alibi.

Katie promised that she would not say too much and they sat down to supper.

As Tuesday night rolled around, Katie almost called Mr. Thomson and told him that she would not be able to make the meeting. She was afraid of being put in the very precarious position of either telling what she knew, or all they thought she knew, which was not much more than the rest of them, or keeping her mouth shut to protect her friendship with Joe.

As she approached the Greenbrier Mansion, she was again awe struck as she always was by its beauty.

Katie heard the chimes of the grand wall clock that hung in the huge entrance room strike nine as she walked through the beautifully carved double entrance doors. Oh God, she was late to her very first meeting, she thought, as the chiming stopped.

Katie hurried through the library doors and all heads turned as she entered the room. For the second time in her life, she felt like turning and running. This was so unusual a feeling for her to have that she started to think she was getting old.

As she took her seat, she gazed around at the faces of the other members sitting in the room. It did not surprise her that one was noticeably missing. Of course, Tom Crook was not present; after all, he was still in mourning.

Katie sat in her designated seat, the one that would be hers until the day that she died or became too feeble-minded to hold. Once you had gained admittance to the club, you were there forever. No one had ever lost his or her place at the huge oval table and Katie hoped that she would not be the first.

"Well, here is our newest member," Mr. Thomson said glancing at his watch. "I remember you being much more punctual when you were in high school than you seem to be now."

Katie's face turned as red as a beet. She stammered her apologies; her watch must be running a bit behind.

Mr. Thomson shrugged the excuse off. "I am quite sure that you won't let it happen again," he said looking down his nose at her.

They ran the meeting according to Roberts Rules of Order. After all of the old and new business was taken care of, the meeting went to the issue that was uppermost in everyone's mind.

Without any preamble, Colonel Simons stated, "I know how this murder was committed. Of course I am going to keep it to myself so that I don't ruin the fun for everyone else."

The pompous ass, Katie thought. He was going to take credit even if the whole group figured out what had happened.

Mr. Thomson gave him a scathing look and announced that they would solve the murder as a group and that no single person would be accredited with solving it.

"I think that Katie Scarlett should be put in charge of doing all the leg work that will need to be done, " Mrs. Finch said. "After all she is the youngest member of the group, and the rest of us won't have to be running around trying to obtain phone records and things while we have her here to do it." She gave Brenda a purposeful look as she said this.

Now how had she heard there were phone records that needed to be checked out? Joe had told George and Katie, in strictest confidence, that indeed there had been a phone call made. This call, he told them, gave Tom Crook an airtight alibi. Somehow, Mrs. Finch had gotten hold of this information and was putting her in a spot that Katie did not much like.

Everyone agreed to this when it came to a vote. Brenda wanted to oppose, but was outnumbered.

Katie sat there not knowing how she felt. She was elated that they would all feel she could accomplish what they may not be able to, but on the other hand when it came down to leg work she was the only member of the group whose legs could still get them around without too much difficulty.

Katie was ashamedly caught up in their enthusiasm of trying to solve the case. Even though she had the greatest respect for Joe's abilities, she reminded herself that as one of a group of mystery buffs, it would not hurt if they could lend him a hand.

"What is the latest word from the chief?" Brenda asked as she glared at Katie.

She was drilling through Katie with her eyes, making Katie very uncomfortable.

"I do know that there was a phone call made at 9:20 AM to Jane Hasting from Ann on the day of her death," Katie said with confidence. "You know Jane and her husband Jim live next door to the Crooks. They are the ones with the six kids."

"Do go on," the group in unison urged her.

"Yes, there was a phone call to the Hasting residence that was picked up by their answering machine at exactly 9:20 AM. Their answering machine is correct in the time, this has been checked on." Oh, she was getting herself in deeper by the minute, but as she looked at Brenda she just couldn't stop herself. She had to wipe that smirk off Brenda's face. Katie wanted her to know that she did have friends and that not everyone thought of her as Brenda did, as some horrible creature, or however it was that Brenda thought of her.

Katie went on with confidence. "The police know that Tom was at a business meeting with no less than five other men at the exact time the phone call was placed, and that he never left the building until he was summoned home by the police. So he couldn't possibly have been the one that killed Ann."

Colonel Simons said, "I told you that Katie would be invaluable to us. We should have gotten her into our little group years before this."

"What else do you know?" asked Mr. Thomson.

"I know that Mrs. Hasting wasn't at home at the time the phone call came in," she was taking the youngest of the Hastings children to day care, as she did every morning at that time."

"Was the time that she did this everyday a well-known fact?" the Colonel asked.

"I'm not sure. You would certainly think that Ann knew this since she lived right next door."

"Doesn't that seem odd?" Mrs. Finch spoke up. "I mean why Mrs. Crook would wait until Mrs. Hasting was gone to call her. After all, she did not make it a habit to hide her disgust of her neighbors, their children, and their pets. She never made any bones about telling anyone exactly how she felt about them." You could hear the quiver in her voice as she said this. She must have been thinking of her poor little dog, Baby.

"Exactly what was said in the phone call?" Katie was asked.

"It seems that Ann said, 'Jane, those kids of yours better stay off of my lawn or else.'"

"Nothing else was said? She didn't give her name or anything?" Mrs. Finch asked Katie.

"I think that was it. After all, since she had made numerous threats to Jane she more than likely didn't have to state her name."

"It's still odd. You would think she'd have said something like, 'This is Ann Crook,' and then made the statement," observed Mr. Thomson.

"I may not be repeating it verbatim, but that was the gist of the conversation."

"Katie, we need to know what was said word for word, so that is a little assignment for you," Brenda said with a smile. She thought she was being smart by trying to put Katie in a corner to see how much she could really find out.

Katie smiled back and said that she did know the call had been made from Ann Crook's cell phone and not the house phone. There, take that, Brenda, she thought.

"How do you know that?" Brenda asked.

Katie had already dipped her toes in so she may as well jump in with both feet. "You do know that George and I," she emphasized this statement, "are friends with Chief Taylor, don't you, Brenda?" She could have cut her own tongue out as soon as the words left her mouth, but she could not let this woman get the better of her.

"I guess that we can depend on you to keep us up to date then, can't we?" Brenda said.

Damn her and damn my big mouth, Katie thought.

The chimes in the entrance hall chimed eleven times. It was time for the meeting to end. They agreed to have another meeting in one week instead of waiting for next month.

Katie promised that she would find out everything she could, as did the rest of the group, and they made their departures.

As they were leaving the mansion, Mr. Thomson spoke everyone's thoughts when he said, "We have to find out everything we can and especially who gave Ann the wine. Now that Tom is off the suspect list, they will have to come up with a likely person to take his place. As we all know everyone hated Ann, and any of us could fill the bill." A truer statement had never been made, as they would soon find out.

As Mrs. Finch and Katie made their way through the darkness towards their homes Katie prophesied, "Now there is going to be a second murder in the village."

"Whatever do you mean, dear?" Mrs. Finch gave her an inquiring look.

"When I tell George what I have done tonight he is going to strangle me," she said with a sigh. "At least there will be no doubt as to the identity of the murderer this time. They'll have to pry George's fingers from my throat."

Mrs. Finch gave a little twitter of a laugh and said, "Nonsense George would never kill you; on the other hand you may want to keep your distance from Chief Taylor for awhile."

"Unfortunately it's George and Joe's bowling night tomorrow, so I will have to face him," Katie lamented.

"Oh, I am sure that everyone knows everything that has happened to this point anyway. So he can't really be too upset with you, can he?"

Katie dropped Mrs. Finch off at the doorstep of her gorgeous pink with white trim two-story Victorian. The intricate gingerbread trim that adorned the old Victorian had been painted a dark fuchsia, making the house appear as if it were a giant dollhouse. It was one of the loveliest homes in Greenbrier and had even been featured on the Simmons Post Gazette gardening page for its breathtaking landscaping. The home had every type of flower you could possibly imagine growing inside the boundaries of its white picket fence. Mrs. Finch's goldfish ponds were the envy of everyone within a 150-mile radius. After taking in the beauty of Mrs. Finch's home, as Katie always did, she walked next door to her own.

George and Katie also lived in a gorgeous Victorian home. It was not quite as ostentatious as Mrs. Finch's, for they had painted theirs in more muted shades. They had chosen a clay color for the siding and accented the trim with blue and burgundy. They were still in the developmental stages of their gardening and some day hoped that their Japanese koi and goldfish ponds would be a contender for the Greenbrier Water Gardening Club award. George was constantly improving the landscape with small arched Japanese bridges, hand carved benches, and the many birdhouses that he had made. The water gardens were so visually pleasing with their waterfalls and lighting, especially at night, that it gave you a peaceful feeling just walking through them.

When Katie walked in the door, she told Good Old George what she had done at the meeting. He gave her that look that only a husband can and said, "Damn it, Katie, Joe spoke to us in confidence, and the first time you get the chance you tell all."

"Well, not the very first time," she said in defense of herself. "I could have said something as long as a week ago at the diner," she stated sheepishly.

"Honey, I know that it's hard for you to keep quiet, but I really think since Joe is such a close friend you should respect his wishes and not go around telling everyone what he has told us in confidence," George said as he took her in to his arms and held her close.

"Well, Brenda goaded me into it." This was the only defense she could come up with at the moment.

The next night when Joe came to pick George up, Katie told him what she had done.

To her great surprise, he erupted into a great laugh from deep inside of him and said, "You mean that it took you this long to let the cat out of the bag, Katie?" He then gave George a wink and said, "I guess I win the bet."

"Bet? What bet?" She looked from one to the other of them.

"George and I had a little wager, Katie." He was trying not to laugh at the expression on her face. "George was absolutely certain that you would have slipped up in the first week. I on the other hand said it would be a little longer than that for my Katie to let it out."

Katie gave George a scathing look and then laughed. Who would know her better than her wonderful husband other than one of her best friends? They both knew how difficult it was for her to keep a secret.

She recalled the last surprise birthday party they'd thrown for their daughter Rachel. Katie had inadvertently left the menu for the party out in plain sight where Rachel had found it. The closeness to her birthday and the inclusion of all her favorite foods had been a dead give away to Rachel. Katie had become so tongue tied when Rachel had questioned her about the menu that she knew without a doubt what was up.

Then there was the time they'd bought the second-hand car for their second son, Joe, named after Police Chief Joe. Katie had let the cat out of the bag on that occasion by asking him to go out to the garage to get her a case of canning jars. The car was already parked in the garage, and the more she tried to lie about whose car it was, the more she fumbled. She finally had to admit that it was his.

Katie knew that these two wonderful men, who she truly loved, were thinking the same thoughts as she. Nevertheless, to make a bet as to when she would slip up was rather an insult.

"I hope that the other team beats the pants off of you guys tonight," she said with a laugh.

They were still laughing as they walked down the front walk. Katie could see George reaching into his pocket to make good on the bet that they had made. She could only hope that it cost him plenty.

Katie spent the evening watching old mystery movies. That was one of her favorite pastimes when the boys went bowling. She kept hoping that something in one of them would give her a clue as to the murderer's identity. Of course, this did not happen, but she enjoyed her night alone anyway.

A couple of nights later, George and Katie decided to go to Ann's wake. She had been a neighbor after all and they felt obligated to attend.

As Katie was getting dressed in a black pantsuit, George entered the bedroom. "I really don't want to go you know," he said with an odd expression on his face.

"It's not my favorite thing to do either, but what choice do we have," she said as she straightened his tie noticing it was the one Rachel had given him last Christmas.

"We are probably going to be the only ones there with the exception of her family. Let's make it as quick as we can, okay." George hated wakes, and she could tell that he would rather be doing anything else in the world.

"George, you can't be serious. The place will be packed to overflowing if I know anything about the residents of Greenbrier," Katie said with one more tug on his tie.

"There may be a couple of lookie Lous, but I doubt if too many will show up," George said as he pulled his suit jacket on.

As they approached the funeral home, her prediction proved correct. The parking lot was so full that people were parking on both sides of the street from the funeral parlor all the way down to the theater. They ended up having to walk a half a block after parking the car.

"You sure do know people, Katie. I was certain that as hated as that woman had been no one would bother to show up."

"It's human nature for people to be curious. They all want to see a murdered person, and I am quite sure they will all be looking for the murderer as well."

"As far as I'm concerned they won't have to look too far. He'll be standing in the front of the line, thanking the mourners for attending," George said as they entered the foyer of the funeral home.

"So you think that it's Tom, too?" Katie said as George put his arm around her waist.

"I sure do. I don't care what kind of alibi he has. I think that something is being missed somewhere."

He opened the door for her and they entered the beautifully decorated parlor. Katie had been commissioned to do the painting in the parlor after the owner had seen her work at Greenbrier Mansion. It had turned out so well that she'd been hired by two other funeral parlors in neighboring Simmons to decorate for them.

As they approached the family to offer their condolences, Katie immediately saw that Tom's daughters were not present. This really did not surprise her. Everyone knew of the animosity between them and their stepmother. Tom was standing with Ann's daughters thanking the people for attending. He had on a black suit that he'd apparently owned for quite sometime, since it was definitely out of style. As they approached him, Katie noticed that there was not any sign that he'd been crying. This seemed very odd to her. She hoped that if she preceded George in death, he would at least be able to muster a few tears so that people would think he had feelings for her. They told the family how sorry they were and then approached the casket.

Ann looked the same in death as she had in life. Actually, Katie thought, she looked a bit better. She did not have any flowers, with the exception of the spray from her children across her feet. Katie could not believe it; Tom had not even bothered to buy flowers.

As she looked at Ann's thin figure, covered by a white satin blanket, she again thought how gaunt Ann had been. What really caught her eye were Ann's hands. Her long bony fingers, always adorned by numerous diamond and emerald rings, were now bare with the exception of a single gold band on her left hand. Katie felt someone come up beside her. She knew it was Tom without even looking.

"Didn't Jim do a wonderful job on my lovely wife, Katie?"

"Yes, it looks as if she's sleeping," Katie stammered.

"I wish my daughters could have made it in for the funeral, but they are very busy with their business just now."

Katie thought that this was not much of an excuse to miss your stepmother's funeral, but who was she to say.

"She looks so peaceful, doesn't she? I'm going to miss her," he went on in a somber voice.

"I'm sure you will." Katie couldn't even come up with a logical reason for him doing so, such as Ann having been such a wonderful woman, so she just stood there. Though they were surrounded by a room full of people, Katie felt as if they were the only ones present. It was an overwhelming feeling that frightened her for some unknown reason.

"I just noticed that she isn't wearing her rings that she usually wore," Katie blurted out.

"No, I didn't think there was any use putting them on her, and then having to take them back off before we buried her." He said this as if they were discussing the weather instead of his dead wife.

"Oh, I realize that, but I have never seen her without them," Katie said.

"She didn't have them on when she died, so I didn't want them to get lost or anything. You know how things have a way of disappearing." His voice was becoming a bit edgy now.

Katie knew immediately that he was lying to her. She had never seen Ann without the rings in the years since they had moved to Greenbrier. Katie had even gone to Ann's house one day to get donations for their hospital rummage sale and had interrupted her cleaning her already immaculate stove. As she had removed the rubber gloves from her hands, Katie had noticed that she was wearing the rings. She had asked her why she had not removed them while working with such an abrasive chemical as oven cleaner. Ann had told her then that she had never taken them off since her grandmother had given them to her, except to clean them once a week and then she replaced them immediately. She had looked almost sentimental when she told Katie this. Katie had heard that her grandmother had raised her from the time that Ann was a year old and that she had given Ann the rings on her deathbed.

Katie persisted, "She didn't have the rings on when she died? That is so sad. She really seemed to love them, since she always wore them."

"She never wore the rings when she went in the hot tub. She was afraid that they may get ruined," he said in such an abrupt manner that Katie felt she'd better drop the subject.

They spoke for a few more minutes about how much he would miss Ann. As they stood there, Katie noticed the distinct smell of cigarette smoke on his old suit. That was strange; she had never seen Tom smoke. Perhaps he had taken the habit up after Ann's death. She again told him how sorry they were before hurriedly walking away. She went to find George, who had nonchalantly disappeared at the start of her and Tom's conversation.

"Where did you go?" she asked him when she finally found him and Joe standing off to the side of the room.

"Katie, what did you want me to do? You started to give the man the third degree at his wife's wake for God's sake. I felt so uneasy that I had to get out of there."

"Something is definitely up," Katie said unabashed at the disapproval in George's tone.

"Honey, I'm only saying that it really isn't the time or place to be asking him questions. As a matter of fact you have no right to be asking him anything at all; that's Joe's job, not yours."

"I'm sorry, but the man is lying through his teeth, and I want to know why." Joe and George both gave her a look that would have shut most people up, but she persisted.

"When I asked him about Ann's rings the ones that she had gotten from her grandmother, he told me that she never wore them when she went in the hot tub. I know that's a lie. She had told me once that she never took them off except to clean them."

"Maybe she took them off when she went into the tub so the chemicals wouldn't ruin them." This came from Joe.

She told them about her wearing the rings even when she cleaned her oven. "A woman doesn't do things like that," she stated emphatically. "If she wears the rings while cleaning, and states that she never removes them, then she doesn't all of a sudden change."

"Did she have the rings on when she was found Joe?" Katie asked.

"No she didn't. I know that for sure because before we knew the cause of death I was treating the case as suspect, so I asked Tom about the rings. Yes, Katie believe it or not, women are not the only ones who notice things like that. When I saw she didn't have them on, I thought that someone may have killed her for them."

"What did he tell you when you asked?" Katie went on with great persistence.

"He told me the same thing he just told you. She never wore them in the hot tub and she had probably put them in her jewelry box."

"Well, didn't you ask him to check, Joe?"

"The man's wife just died, Katie. I didn't feel it was proper to push the issue. I was sure that if they were missing, he would have come to the station to inform us."

"There's something very odd going on here, don't you think?" Katie had a very uneasy feeling about the whole ring business.

"Katie, please just let it alone," George said.

"I will as soon as I find out where those rings went," she stated stubbornly.

"Just let Joe do his job. I know when you get that Sherlock Holmes look, you think you're on to something, but, like I said, this isn't the time or the place."

Katie got that feeling everyone gets when someone is staring at the back of his or her head. When she turned around to see who it was giving her this creepy feeling, she saw that it was Tom. He was giving her a look that clearly showed he knew they were discussing him.

"There are Ann's daughters. I think I'll go over and talk to them." George immediately stopped her by grabbing her hand before she could make a move.

"You will do no such thing." She was getting the George look that meant that she had better let it drop, so she did. At least, for the time being, that was. Katie tried to give George her most innocent look, which usually worked. She could read in George's face that it wasn't working this time.

As Katie scanned the many faces that filled the room, she spotted Mrs. Finch. Mrs. Finch caught her eye and motioned to Katie to join her.

"I'm going to go over and see Mrs. Finch." This came out more abruptly than she had intended.

"Please, Katie, just stay away from Ann's family." George's eyes were pleading with her.

"I won't go near them," she promised as she turned and made her way to Mrs. Finch's side.

She could hear George sigh deeply as she walked away.

"Hello, Katie Scarlett. Did you come to try to find out the identity of the murderer like everyone else dear?"

"No," Katie stammered. "I just thought that since Ann had been a neighbor, it was the proper thing to do."

"Nonsense, dear. No one would be here if it were not for the fact that she was murdered. I mean no one liked her and we are all very curious, aren't we?"

Katie could not deny this fact. The place would be like a cave if Ann had succumbed in any other way.

"Is that why you're here?" Katie asked.

"Of course it is, Katie Scarlett. Everyone knows that I detested the woman. I just thought I might be able to pick up some clues if I came, you know us amateur sleuths, dear. We always believe that we will be the one that solves the case." Her eyes twinkled as she said this.

"Have you discovered anything yet?" Mrs. Finch asked as they moved to some corner seats.

Katie told her about the rings, and she agreed that this was something that should be investigated.

"It really is rather sad, you know. I mean with the exception of her family, no one is here except to nib nose," Katie said.

"Katie Scarlett, you know the woman was the most vindictive horrible person that ever took a breath. You can't feel bad for her now that she has gotten what she deserved."

"Perhaps she had some redeeming qualities that none of us ever saw."

"She didn't have any good qualities, of that I can assure you, and she is exactly where she should be."

Katie had never heard Mrs. Finch sound so bitter.

"Where do you think she went?" Katie asked sincerely.

"Katie Scarlett, she went where all people like her go, of course. The only thing I can't quite figure out is who was watching hell while she was on this earth."

"Mrs. Finch!" Katie exclaimed.

"Don't try to make her in to some kind of saint just because she is dead now, Katie Scarlett. You feel exactly same way; you're just too kind-hearted to say it."

This was true. She had always been a protector of the underdog. It was just her nature, but Katie still had a hard time thinking that anyone could be so hated that no one cared that she was dead.

"I think that I'll go over and give the girls my condolences."

"Please don't, Mrs. Finch. George will know that I told you about the rings, and he will be furious with me. He told me not to go near them," Katie said in a pleading voice.

"Nonsense, Katie Scarlett. George may be able to tell you what to do, but I am not under his jurisdiction, or anyone's for that matter."

She turned and made her way to Ann's daughters' side before Katie could stop her.

George's eyes caught hers across the room and she instinctively knew she was in big trouble when they got home.

When Mrs. Finch returned to her side, she looked like the cat that swallowed the canary.

"I nonchalantly mentioned the rings to the girls, and according to them the rings are in Ann's jewelry case." There was a slight pause before she went on in a sly little voice. "That is they are all there except for one. They said that Tom had told them he thought Ann had taken one of them to the jeweler to get it repaired. What do you think of that?" she said in a triumphant little whisper.

Katie's mind was racing as she stood there.

"Let's keep this under our hats for awhile and do a little sleuthing on our own, Katie Scarlett. I think that if the two of us put our heads together we will be able to solve this little puzzle, don't you?"

God only knows why, but Katie agreed to this.

The next week she was working another five-day stretch. Terrie approached her with the strangest look on her face.

"You have a phone call," Terrie said. The worried look made furrows across her forehead.

"I never get phone calls at work, only if there's an emergency," Katie gasped. Her stomach first jumped up in to her throat and then her heart dropped to her feet.

"Is it bad news?" She asked Terrie.

"I don't know, hon. It's George. He sounded very serious."

Katie made her way to the phone with a sick feeling in the pit of her stomach.

"George, what is it? Are the kids alright?" she asked in a shaky voice.

His answer shocked her to her very core.

"Brenda has been arrested for the murder of Ann Crook. She is in the county lockup, and she wants to talk to you."

"How could this happen?" Katie's head was whirling. "Why does she want to talk to me?"

"The only thing I could get out of her was that she was arrested because someone said they saw her taking a bottle of wine into the Crook's house the night before the murder, and as we know Ann was poisoned with wine laced with antifreeze. You better go over to the jail as soon as you get off work and see what she wants."

"I want you to go with me," Katie said in a pleading voice.

"I'll pick you up out front of the hospital at three," he said.

The rest of the afternoon went by in a complete haze. Being a med nurse is not one of the easiest things in the world. It was much more difficult with the pressure that Katie had been under these last couple of weeks.

She was going to be face to face with Brenda in a couple of hours, and she did not know what it was that Brenda wanted from her.

Katie had never been to the jail to visit anyone before and she was finding the experience quite overwhelming.

She was taken to the room where suspects were questioned. On the wall was a large mirror, which anyone who had ever watched a police show would recognize immediately as a two-way mirror. There could be no other reason to have such a large mirror in the room except for the purpose for which it was intended, Katie thought.

The guard brought Brenda to the room, and for the first time in her life, Katie felt sorry for her. She had on handcuffs and an orange county lockup jumper. Orange definitely was not her color. It made her look paler and even more washed out than usual. They removed the handcuffs and Brenda sat in the chair across from Katie.

"Brenda, I am so sorry," Katie said

"I just bet you are," she replied.

"No really, if there is anything that I can do to help."

"Well, believe it or not, there is. You can get me out of here."

This statement took Katie back. "George and I aren't rich, but perhaps we could take up a collection and try to get you out on bail."

The look Brenda gave her said louder than words what she felt for her.

"I don't want you to bail me out, you twit. I want you to figure out who the real killer is so that I can get out of here and still hold my head up in public. I don't want to walk around the rest of my life with people's suspicions following me, hounding me like a dog."

"How did they come to arrest you?" Katie asked as she scanned Brenda's tired face.

"They say my fingerprints are all over the wine bottle found at the murder scene. I don't know how this could be, unless someone lifted my prints somehow and put them on it." Brenda sat there stonily.

"Everyone knew that I couldn't stand that woman. Why would I take her a bottle of wine? And if that isn't bad enough," she went on, "they have that old drunk Dick Carlson to testify that he saw me the night before the murder walking toward the Crook's house carrying a bottle of wine. They told me he definitely knows what the local liquor store bags look like, and that it was definitely me with the bag."

There was a slight pause before she went on.

"I did buy a bottle of white wine the day before the murder. I was having company that night for dinner, and I was serving fish." Brenda was very tired; Katie could see it in her eyes.

"I can't believe they trust the word of that old drunk Carlson." She shook her head. "Most of the time he is so drunk he doesn't know what month it is, and they are going to take his word on this."

"I don't think they would necessarily believe him over you, but if they found your fingerprints on the bottle, that is pretty damning evidence, Brenda."

"That is what is bothering me the most. I went to the liquor store, picked out a bottle of wine and then went home. How can my fingerprints be on the wine bottle that contained the antifreeze?"

"You should get an attorney right away," Katie told her.

"They got the public defender, Ben Cooper, for me. With him as a lawyer, I will be in the gas chamber before the end of the year. You know the only reason there are lawyers is that there are lawyers. I have absolutely no faith in the judicial system in this village. You know that all of these lawyers are in bed together."

Katie had found this out personally when the Crooks had gone to court against George. Tom had said it would be a slam-dunk case because he had done favors for everyone involved. The way it worked out, Katie knew this to be true. George lost the case because Tom had done so many favors for so many people. She had even found out that Tom's lawyer, who Tom called the biggest thief in the county, had falsified some deeds at the courthouse so that one of his clients ended up with a piece of land that had originally been deeded to the village years before. How could any honest person win in a situation such as that?

"What do you want me to do?" Katie asked.

"Even though we haven't always seen eye to eye on too many things in the past,"—this was the understatement of the year Katie thought—"I have great faith in your deductive reasoning. If anyone can get me out of here you can," Brenda sighed. Katie thought she would probably never forget her next words. "You do owe me you know? You did steal my precious fiancé away from me after all."

Katie did not want to remind Brenda, that she and George had never been engaged. She thought this would push her over the edge given Brenda's current state of mind.

"I'm not promising anything, but I'll see what I can do."

"Just remember if I'm found guilty, it will be your fault. Yours and nobody else's," Brenda said as she looked deep into Katie's eyes.

After their conversation, Katie left the building almost in a run. When she got into the car, she told George everything that had transpired.

He apologized for not going in with her, but Brenda had made it very clear that she had wanted to see Katie alone.

When they got home, George went up to take a shower and Katie snuck out back to have a cigarette. Katie knew that she should definitely know better than to smoke, but at times, she felt smoking was a security blanket. She had smoked when George and she first met, but had quit after his continuous nagging about her habit. Now as she drew the smoke into her lungs, she could feel the calming effect that it brought to her. George never said too much about her smoking if they were with a group of people that also smoked, especially if they were having a beer or two. He would be very upset though if he thought she was going to start smoking on a steady basis again. Of course, she did not plan to do so, at least not now.

Her thoughts were going in many directions as she stood in the freezing night air. The frost-covered trees appeared as if they were encrusted with thousands of tiny diamonds as the back porch light illuminated them.

Katie had figured out many a mystery in her life, especially the ones at the Halloween parties. She had even convinced the ACDC that O.J. could have dropped the glove at his home after the murders of Nicole and Ron. This was different though. This murder had happened in her own backyard, and the people involved were all well known to her. Some of them were very close indeed. What hung heaviest over her was the she did feel as if she owed it to Brenda to try to solve this case. Brenda had never married after Katie and George had gotten together. As far as Katie knew, she had never even dated. Had she really ruined Brenda's life? Katie's mind was troubled as she stood in the freezing night air. On the other hand, was she taking the blame for something that was out of her control?

The next morning on her way to work Katie's mind was so full of the case that she could think of nothing else. The first thing she had to do was figure out who really committed the murder. This would be a daunting task. After all, so many people had wanted to see Ann Crook dead.

Just because the police had ruled out her husband, Tom, was not good enough for Katie. He was still on her list of suspects. The police could have missed something, and Katie would be like a bloodhound on the trail to see what it could be.

There was also old Mrs. Finch. To look at her you would not have thought that she could kill a fly. On the other hand, she had hated Ann with such a passion after what had happened to Baby that she could have mustered up the courage to exact her revenge on the woman. What sweet revenge it would be, Katie thought. For her to take this woman's life in the same way that her precious little dog's had been taken would be the ultimate revenge.

Colonel Simons could also be put on the list of suspects. Ann had not only bought many of his family heirlooms for a ridiculously low price, she had then rubbed it in by selling a few of the items for an exorbitant amount of money. She had mentioned this no less than five times that Katie knew of in front of many witnesses. This had to have made him very angry. Could he have been angry enough to kill her? Katie doubted it, but you never know what is in another person's mind.

Even Jane and Jim Hasting could have had good reason to want her dead. They had lived in the neighborhood for approximately ten years before the Crooks arrived. They had never had any problems with anyone to Katie's knowledge before these hateful people moved in. Once the Crooks moved in, their whole life was turned upside down. The police had been called at least two times a week for the most trivial matters. If their children were walking past the Crook house and their feet just touched the edge of the grass, Ann Crook would immediately call the police with a complaint of trespassing.

The police were also called when the Hastings would have a get together in their backyard, even though no one else in the neighborhood thought they were being too loud. Of course, most of the neighbors were invited to join these gatherings, with the obvious exception of the Crooks. They had lived in the perfect neighborhood and now they lived in hell. Katie could not picture Jane, who was all of five feet two inches tall, slim, with auburn hair, harming anyone. She was such a great mom and a wonderful person that it would be totally out of character for her. On the other hand, threatening harm to one of her brood would be like getting between a mother bear and her cub. It would be a deadly place to be. The most deadly place on earth.

Then there was Jane's husband, Jim. Jim Hasting was a young man that everyone liked. He was very protective of his family, but Katie couldn't picture him harming anyone. If it were one of them, Katie would put her money on Jane.

It was well-known that Ann definitely did not like the Hastings children. When the Crooks first bought the old Victorian Ann had all the old spruce trees, which seemed to reach the heavens topped. It was rumored that Ted the eldest of the Hastings and Ned, the second oldest, were there as the trees had their beautiful bows cut away. Ned had asked his older brother why anyone would do this, and Ted had answered, "I think it's to give the old witch broom clearance." Several people had been standing about at the time this remark was made, and the little story quickly ended up reaching Ann's ears. She was heard to say, "If either of those two boys ever walks on my property again, they will never walk off." This became rather a game with the freckled-face little boys, and it seemed they would do anything just to irritate Ann after this.

Old man Thomson also had an axe to grind with Ann. She had made a mortal enemy of him by publicly embarrassing him at the Founder's Day celebration, which was held every May. She stated that she had heard through the grapevine that he had shown inappropriate behavior towards several of his female students over the years. This of course outraged not only him, but also all of his former students and most of the town. To have a teacher of his background accused of something like that could have ruined him completely. Even though he no longer taught school, it had put a black mark on his immaculate record as an educator. The whole town knew that she was lying. Nevertheless, once this was said, mothers started to warn their daughters not to become too chummy with Mr. Thomson, just in case there was any truth to these rumors.

Then, of course, there was George. Katie should be ashamed for even thinking such a thing, but he did hate the woman. When he had to sue to get the money that the Crooks owed him for all of the work he'd done on their Victorian it had upset him to the core. He had never had a complaint about his workmanship in the thirty years he'd been a contractor. It was not so much Tom who was the problem, but Ann, who had made so many changes as the work progressed that the extras went way above what Tom had been willing to pay for. Ann said that the house had to be perfect, and it was on completion. When Tom was given the final bill, he would not, or could not pay for all of the extras that Ann had demanded. Ann had called Katie, and with a great many vulgarities had demanded that George come to the house to see all of the mistakes he and his sub-contractors had made. Up until that point, Ann had bragged about George's talents, but now she exclaimed how disappointed she was with his workmanship. Tom of course did not have any backbone at all; he would listen to anything this horrible woman said and do her bidding.

Katie had even jokingly said to Ann at one point that Tom was going to divorce her if she spent any more money on the house. Ann had laughed and said. "That wimp won't ever divorce me, Katie. Ever since he divorced that other woman that he had been married to, he would never divorce me because I would ruin him." Of course, she had used such profanity while saying this that Katie would never even repeat it.

When George went to court, both Ann and Tom blatantly lied to such an extent that it astounded George and Katie. George ended up not being paid any of the actual cost, he had in the house. Since the Crooks were such habitual liars, the judge had believed much of what they'd said. Then again, it could have been as Tom claimed that the judge was in his pocket. He had stated many times that if he ever went to court in front of the judge they had, it would be a slam-dunk case. He had told many people that the judge owed him for favors that he had done for him while he was in office, and that the judge owed him big time. On the other hand, it could have been because Tom's lawyer was such a cheat, and was known to do illegal things, such as falsify deeds, and the like. Tom had even made the statement that his lawyer, Chris Barker, was the biggest thief in the county. Of course, that was before he had hired him to defend him in this matter.

Ann and Tom could not leave well enough alone. They would say to anyone that would listen that they were going to ruin Katie's husband's business and her career, also. They would bad mouth the two of them whenever they could. Tom of course having very little backbone would let Ann make the wads and he would throw them. Katie often thought that this is what happens when you are married to an overbearing, nagging woman such as she was.

As George said before the judgment was made, "Katie no matter what happens I will be the winner. After all I will still be married to you, and he will have to be married to that horrible bitch for the rest of their lives." Of course, he had never thought that this would turn out to be such a very short time.

There were also Tom's daughters, who held great animosity toward their wicked stepmother. Ann would be pleasant enough to their faces, in front of Tom, and then she would call them every unladylike name in the book behind their backs. Unladylike really was not a strong enough way of putting it. She had the most vulgar mouth that anyone could imagine. You would never hear a real lady or any woman worth her while use the vulgarities that passed through Ann's lips. She had told Katie on numerous occasions that Tom's daughters may have to come and sit at her table for holidays and the like, "but they will never stay in my house." It was always her house, never her and Tom's.

Katie would have to investigate as to when either of Tom's daughters had last come for a visit. Ann was not only horrible to them, but she had a hatred for their children, who were only one and two years old. She would make statements about Tom's granddaughter such as "that ugly little freak will never be as precious and gorgeous as my little Kimberly is." Kimberly was her only granddaughter. This had upset Katie so badly that she wouldn't even stop to see George the final six weeks that he was working on that woman's house. This would also be reason enough for Tom's daughters to hate her. Katie would have to find a way to see if they had visited just before the murder.

Of course, not all of the blame for their horrible marriage could be placed on Ann's doorstep. Tom was no better than she was. When it came to Ann's children from a previous marriage, Tom had been heard to say that Ann's youngest was "a leech that he was sick and tired of footing the bills for," and that she was nothing, but "a suicidal alcoholic."

The more Katie thought about it, the more she thought that these two people had truly deserved one another.

She could go on forever listing the people who had reasons to hate Ann. She would have to start with those that had means, opportunity, and motive, closest to home first.

When Katie arrived at the hospital, the first person she met was Terrie. She asked her what had happened on her visit with Brenda, and Katie gave her all of the details.

"Oh God, Katie," Terrie said aghast. "How does that woman, who has been so mean spirited towards you for all of these years, expect you to solve this case?"

"Well, she believes that since I solved a few mysteries here and there, I can do the same in this case."

"You do have one of those minds that can grasp details that the rest of us wouldn't ever see. I mean you did convince the ACDC of how the Simpson case could have been solved."

"That was all assumption on my part. Moreover, it was not like a murder in your own village the way this one is. I feel as if I am entirely too close to all of the suspects in this case. I mean anyone that I know could have committed this murder, even you," Katie said looking at her friend.

"You really don't think that it was me, do you? Not that I liked the woman or anything, but I really didn't have a motive."

"Well, you're about the only one that didn't," Katie said with sincerity.

They promised to eat lunch together so that Katie could tell her everything she had thought of thus far. Katie always bounced ideas off Terrie when she found herself stumped. Terrie would be very honest with her. Not being as involved in this mess as Katie unfortunately was, she may see things that Katie was missing, Katie thought.

The next person she encountered was Doc Campbell.

They discussed a few of their patients' medical problems and then she asked him.

"Doctor, how much antifreeze would it take to kill a person?"

"It all depends on how recently the person had eaten, of course. If they had consumed a very large dinner for instance, it would take quite a bit more antifreeze than say if their stomach were empty." He gave her a searching look and then went on. "If the stomach were empty it would more than likely take a couple of ounces of antifreeze to kill them."

"Could the taste of the antifreeze be detected, as in something like wine?" she asked.

"Antifreeze has a rather syrupy taste I've heard. I believe that wine would more than likely be unable to cover the taste of it."

"Katie, I have a feeling that the sleuth is coming out in you again," he said with a fond smile at her, his fingers combing through his hair as he spoke.

Katie had always liked Doc Campbell. He was very easy going and not in the least arrogant or uppity like many of the other doctors that she had worked with.

Katie told him exactly what she was up to. He smiled and said that with her determination she would be able to crack the case.

This bolstered her self-esteem quite a bit. He was himself one of the most brilliant people Katie had ever met, and he had solved more than one mystery in his day. The ACDC had been trying to induct him into their realm for many years. He would always say that he was just too busy with his career to take the time. This was in all probability true since approximately three quarters of the residents of Greenbrier were his patients.

Katie went on her way. She was feeling a great deal more confident than she had when she walked into the hospital just a few minutes before.

The day went by without any major problems with any of their patients. Katie was going to have three days in a row off and she couldn't wait. She would have to get on the ball if she wanted to get Brenda off and find the real murderer before a trial date was set. Katie would more than likely have plenty of time since the wheels of justice in Greenbrier turned very slowly, Greenbrier not having a sitting judge. They would have to wait until one could be brought in from Wilmer, a little town to the north of them. Nevertheless, with her luck, the judge would have a light calendar and set a date for the trial immediately, Katie thought.

She woke up the next morning very refreshed. The sun was shining through the beautiful stained glass windows of her second floor bedroom. The first thing that she had to do was to go to the police station and find out everything she could about the actual evidence. Katie was not sure if she could gain the information she was seeking from Joe, but she would give it her best shot.

Joe welcomed her into his office with a smile. "What is our little sleuth up to today?' he asked as she sat down in front of his desk.

"I wondered if there was any possibility of me listening to the phone recording that Ann had made to Jane Hasting," she said without any preamble.

"Now, Katie, you know that I really can't give any outsider information like that."

"I just thought that if I could listen to the tape, I may be able to hear something in it that would provide us with some kind of clue. I know that it is probably against policy, but I am asking this as a friend, Joe."

As they spoke, he took a tape recorder out of one of the drawers and sat it on top of his desk. He then said that he had to step out of his office for a few minutes and that he knew that she would not take it upon herself to listen to the tape.

Katie knew this was Joe's way of letting her listen to the tape without him being present.

He excused himself and as soon as he had left the room, her hand, a bit shaky now, reached for the play button. Katie had a paper and pencil handy so that she could write down exactly what was said. She needed it to be word for word, so that there was no question as to the accuracy of what was stated on the tape.

As the tape started to play, it announced the date and time, November 14, 9:20 AM. There was a short pause and then a voice, which she immediately recognized as Ann's. It was quite high pitched, but this was something that Katie had noticed about Ann's voice in the past. Her voice would get rather loud when she was angry, which happened often. The tape said, "Jane better keep those damn brats off of our property, or the police will be called and there will be trespassing charges made." That was it. There was the sound of the phone being hung up and then silence.

When she first heard the tape she thought that this was exactly something that Ann would say while making one of her numerous complaint calls to a neighbor. Katie played the tape repeatedly and listened intently.

She noticed that there were no background noises. It was just that statement and nothing else.

The more she listened to the tape the more she thought it sounded like a statement were being made, to someone as to what Ann was going to say when she called Jane up to warn her children away from her yard. One of the first things that she noticed, after listening more closely, was that there was no pause between the words Jane and better. There were no other words either. You would think that she would have said "Jane YOU better keep those damn brats off of our property." Not just Jane better. There was another odd thing. Ann had not said this is Ann Crook or introduced herself in any way. She had just made this statement and then hung up.

Katie listened to the tape a couple of more times and wrote every word down.

When Joe returned to the room, she was sitting there thinking about what she had just heard.

"Joe, did you notice that Ann didn't pause or say YOU between the words Jane and better?" she asked.

"Didn't I tell you that I couldn't allow you to listen to the tape, Katie?"

"Well, in fact, you didn't let me listen; you were out of the room when I heard it."

He gave her a look and said. "Believe it or not, Katie, we did notice that. We are trained investigators, you know?"

"Don't you think it's odd? I mean it sounds as if she is making a statement as to what she was going to say to Jane, instead of actually talking to her."

"We had the same question. We think that at the time Ann made the phone call, she was either already three sheets to the wind, or that the poison was already taking effect."

"Don't you think that it's odd that it's 9:20 in the morning and she was already drinking?" she persisted.

"According to her husband, Tom, Ann was a closet drinker. He said Ann would start to drink very early in the morning and continue to do so until late in the evening. This could be the reason that she was so antisocial and mean spirited."

This was a well-known fact amongst the locals. They had all seen Ann where she would act in very strange manner. She had been taken to the ER on several occasions after taking a fall from being intoxicated.

"I will tell you what I know so far, off the record of course," he said with a smile towards Katie.

"Ann was seen on November 13th between 8 and 9 PM out walking in her yard. A number of her neighbors verified this. If you remember, she had yelled at a couple of the neighborhood kids as they were walking home from scouts. Tom left the house at 7:50 AM on the 14th. This has also been verified, by speaking to the neighbors. He arrived at his office at 8:AM, where he was having a meeting with a group of men. He was in the meeting with the others until 10:AM. He left the office at approximately 1:PM after receiving the call from us about Ann."

Joe was watching her as he continued with his story. "The gas meter reader had found Ann. He had to go past the sunroom where the hot tub was located to read the meter, and he saw her floating in the hot tub. She was face down in the water. He had first called 911 on his cell phone. We were then notified, and we called Tom's office to summon him home. That was after an initial investigation was performed. We told him that there was an emergency, but didn't specify what it was."

There was another slight pause before Joe continued. "He arrived home at 1:20 PM and was told the news. He took it very hard, of course, and it took some time for us to calm him down."

"We had found the wine bottle, along with others, beside the hot tub. This was when Tom informed us that Ann had been a closet drinker. As you know, we had thought that she had become intoxicated while sitting in the tub, and had fallen asleep and drowned. Since she wasn't under the care of a physician for any grave illness at the time, we had to have an autopsy performed."

"You know what the results of this were. She had ingested a great quantity of antifreeze, since she had drunk the entire bottle, along with a great deal more that morning, and this had caused her death. You pretty much know the rest of the story, Katie." The whole time that Joe was telling the story his eyes never left hers.

"I just can't believe that Ann would have drunk wine when it would have had an odd taste to it," Katie said more to herself than to Joe. "You would think that as soon as she tasted it she would have known that something was wrong with the wine."

"I thought that was odd too. The coroner did say that while doing the autopsy he found an old injury that she had had to her head."

"What do you mean, Joe?"

"He said that some kind of nerve in her head had been damaged years ago, I believe he mentioned a cranial nerve."

"Did he say that it was the trigeminal nerve by chance?"

"Yes it did start with a t, I'm sure that it did."

"If she had damage to the trigeminal nerve that would explain it."

Joe looked baffled and Katie went on to explain. "The Mandibular branch of this particular nerve, when damaged, can cause you to lose the sense of taste."

Joe still looked baffled.

"In other words, Joe, she may not have been able to taste, or detect textures of certain things because of it."

"You would think that someone would have known about her head injury," Joe said. "I mean nothing usually gets by the gossips in this town after all."

"Ann, never mentioned any kind of head injury to me," Katie was thinking aloud once again.

"That really wouldn't be something that a woman like Ann would mention, Katie. She was an extremely vain person after all, and she may not have wanted anyone to know that there was something wrong with her."

"I had always assumed that her speech impediment was due to her overbite, but now that I know about the nerve damage, I could have been mistaken about that."

"I wonder how many people knew about Ann's head injury? Tom would have known for sure," Katie said, as she looked deep into Joe's eyes.

"Yes, he would have known for sure, but I don't think that he would be smart enough to have thought of poisoning her with the wine laced with antifreeze. Another thing Katie, if Tom wanted to kill her, he would have just drowned her, don't you think?"

"If she would have just drowned and there was no wine, then he would have been the top suspect, Joe. This way there are so many suspects because everyone hated her and most homes have a jug of antifreeze somewhere in them, that it took a great deal of the suspicion away from him."

"It really doesn't matter, Katie. The prosecutor has a mound of evidence against Brenda and I'm sure that he will get a conviction."

Katie decided that she had better get the answers to some of the other questions that she had, so she changed to a new topic.

"You say that her cell phone was used to make the call to Jane. Joe, how do you know that it was hers and not someone else's?"

"We found her cell phone at the bottom of the hot tub. It had been smashed, but we figured considering where we found it, that she was more than likely making a phone call around the time of death. When we questioned the neighbors, Jane Hasting said that she had received a call from Ann at 9:20 that very morning on her answering machine."

"We checked with the cell phone provider and they confirmed that the call was placed from Ann's cell phone. They also confirmed the exact time of the call."

"Why would she use her cell phone to make the call?" Katie asked. "She had telephones in every room in her house; I know this because when George worked on the house he had installed them."

"Who's to say, Katie? Perhaps she was already in the hot tub and didn't want to get out to make the call."

"How did you come to find Brenda's fingerprints on the wine bottle, Joe?"

"We were treating the scene as a possible homicide from the get go. We always do this when there is a possibility that what appears to be an accident, really isn't."

"We had bagged the wine bottle as a precautionary measure, and when it was examined by the lab in Simmons, we found the fingerprints."

"Why would you think that they were Brenda's?" she persisted.

"We were questioning everyone within the area at the time of the murder. When we questioned Dick Carlson, who lived five doors down from the Crooks, he mentioned that he had seen Brenda Cormick with a bag from the local liquor store. He also mentioned that she was walking into the Crooks house, the night before the murder. If anyone could identify a bag from the liquor store it would be Dick." Everyone knew this to be a fact since Dick Carlson was known as the town drunk.

"Upon further investigation of the murder, we discovered that the clerk at the liquor store confirmed the fact that Brenda had been there on the evening in question. He also confirmed that she had purchased a bottle of wine. After we brought her in for questioning we fingerprinted her; it was then discovered that her prints matched the ones on the bottle."

"Were there any other prints on the bottle?" Katie was not going to give up.

"Yes, there were those of Ann of course, and also the clerk's. There were some others, but Tom's didn't show up. Brenda's on the other hand were very clear."

"Are you sure that Tom never left the meeting or the building on the day of the murder?" She reverted to this subject.

"We are positive about this fact. Everyone in the building said the same thing. He was there from 8AM until the phone call at approximately 1:10PM."

"Did they take any breaks during the meeting?" Katie asked.

"What would that matter, Katie? He never left the building so he couldn't have killed her."

"Could you check on this for me, Joe?"

"I can check, but it really seems useless. Most of the people in the office dislike Tom, and it would be very unlikely that they would give us false statements to try and protect him if that's what you're thinking."

"One other question Joe. What was Dick Carlson doing home on the night before the murder? He usually sits at the Fox and Hound until closing time."

"We asked him this, knowing his background and all. It would seem that he had been barred from the Fox and Hound for three days. This, we found out was because he had started an argument two days prior to the murder. He had one more night before he would be permitted back in."

This was not at all uncommon, Katie thought. Dick had been kicked out of the pub so many times in the past for the very same thing.

"One other thing, Katie," he said before she had a chance to make her get away. "We found an emerald and diamond ring in Brenda's house when we searched it. It matches the description of the one that Tom said was missing from Ann's jewelry box after the murder."

"I thought he said he knew that it was at the jewelers being repaired?"

"Now where did you hear that may I ask?"

"Mrs. Finch sort of asked Ann's daughters about the ring, and they told her that Tom said he thought that it was being fixed," she blushed as she said this since she hadn't mentioned it to George or Joe the night of the wake.

"He's now saying that he checked with the jeweler and that it hadn't been at his shop."

Katie's mind was racing. She could picture Brenda being angry enough to kill Ann after the underhanded things that she had done to her, but she could never picture Brenda stealing, especially something like one of the ornate emerald and diamond rings Ann had owned. Brenda was a very plain person and would be the last individual to want something as showy as one of Ann's rings.

"Which ring was it, Joe?" Ann had three emerald and diamond rings that were beautiful. Two very large ones had two-carat diamonds with emeralds surrounding the huge stones. There was also the smaller one that was a one-carat square cut diamond, surrounded by emeralds. This had always been Katie's favorite since it was not as gaudy as the larger rings.

"It was the smallest of the three that she wore. It has been identified by Tom."

"Don't you think that if someone was going to murder a person for their jewelry that they would take all of the rings?" she asked him.

"Maybe she thought that if she took the smallest ring that no one would notice that it was missing."

"That's nonsense, Joe. No one could help but notice that a ring of that quality was gone. I just can't believe Brenda would steal one of the rings, Joe."

"The only thing that I can tell you, Katie, is that we found it in a drawer of an antique dresser that was in Brenda's garage."

"Anyone could have put it there you know. I have seen Brenda's garage door open on many occasions when I've passed her house."

"You could be right, but the DA thinks that he has the prime suspect under arrest and he is sure of a conviction."

"We all know about the judicial system in this village, Joe, and I am going to try to prove him wrong," Katie said as she stood up.

"If there is one thing that I'm sure of Brenda didn't murder Ann." At least not for a diamond ring, she thought to herself.

Katie thanked Joe for all of his help and left the police station.

There was so much evidence stacked against Brenda just now that she thought that Joe was more than likely right when he said that the DA was going to get a conviction. Why did she feel so obligated to a woman that had hated her for so many years? She didn't know the answer to this question; she just knew that she had to do everything in her power to get Brenda out of jail.

As she was walking down the street, she encountered Julie, a friend of Tom's daughters, Renee and Sharon. Katie nonchalantly asked her if she had seen the girls just before the murder was committed. She told her that she thought that she had seen one of them in town.

Julie said they absolutely were not in town. "For one thing, Mrs. Adams, they would have stopped in to see me; they always stop in when they are in town. I know that they were both attending a huge convention that entire week out in California for the business that they own. I had talked to Renee the week before and she had told me all about it."

"Oh, so that's why they didn't attend the funeral?" Katie went on.

"You do know that Ann was always very mean to them. Therefore, you really can't blame them for not wanting to be there." She acted as if Katie's questioning was bothering her greatly.

"Yes, I had heard that they didn't get along very well."

"You certainly don't think that they had anything to do with this. Do you?"

"No of course I don't." Her words sounded like a lie even to her own ears.

"I really have to be going," Julie stated in a tone that gave Katie no choice but to end the conversation.

They wished one another happy holidays and Katie went on her way. That took Tom's daughters off her suspect list. At least she was narrowing it down. Katie was sure that Julie would call Tom's daughters and tell them of their conversation, but she had to narrow her list down if she were ever going to come to the correct solution as to which person that hated Ann was her murderer.

Katie's next stop was the liquor store. She knew the clerk, Ken, and he greeted her warmly.

"Ken, can I ask you a couple of questions?" Katie's gaze swept the store, which was very busy at the moment.

"I was wondering when you would be in, Katie."

What am I, the town gossip, or something, Katie thought? Everywhere she went, she was greeted the same way.

"Ken, do you remember the night that Brenda came in to purchase wine?"

"I sure do. As I told the police, it stands out in my memory very well. Miss Cormick rarely comes to the store; she's been here maybe one or at most two times since I've worked here in the last five years."

"Do you remember what she bought when she came in?"

"She bought a bottle of white wine."

This is what Brenda herself had told Katie, so she knew that Brenda's story was accurate.

"Do you remember who else was in the store at the time?"

"It was a Saturday night, and that being our busiest night of the week, with the holidays coming up, the store was packed as usual. I really didn't make it a point to take note of all our customers. Of course I would've been a little bit more observant if I'd have known there was going to be a murder."

"Did you notice if Tom Crook came in?" Katie persisted.

"The police asked me that, and like I told them, Mr. Crook was a frequent customer, so it really wouldn't have stood out in my memory if he had been in here."

Katie was ready to make her departure when she asked. "Did Brenda Cormick say anything that you remember as odd while she was in here?"

"No, she just was having difficulty picking out a wine, so I helped her, that's all."

"What do you mean she was having trouble picking out a wine?" Katie asked her interest peeked.

"She was in the wine section for a good fifteen minutes looking at all the different wines. When I got a chance, I went over and asked her if I could help her. She was holding a bottle of red wine and was examining it carefully. She asked me if it would be a good wine to serve with fish. I told her that you usually served white wine with fish and took her to the white wine section. I picked out a nice little white wine, a Chablis, for her; it is one of my favorites and a bit pricey at thirty dollars a bottle. She made her purchase and then left."

"So you saw her holding a bottle of red wine?"

"I absolutely did. I told her that we have wine classes once a month, and told her that she should join us if she wanted to learn more about wines and which ones to serve with what food. She said that she really wasn't interested, and that she never drank herself. I think that she mentioned she was having guests that night, and that she was only purchasing it because they liked wine with their meals."

"Did you tell Chief Taylor about Brenda looking for a wine?" Katie felt that she was on to something, but was not exactly sure, what.

"It wasn't Chief Taylor that questioned me," he said. "It was his deputy. You know the one that everyone calls Barney Fife."

"Yes, I know, Calvin." He did remind one of Barney from "The Andy Griffith Show". Everyone in Greenbrier even thought that he probably didn't carry a loaded gun, just like Barney on the show. Wasn't it ironic that Chief Taylor had the same name as the character that Andy Griffith portrayed on the show? Katie had never thought of it before.

"Do you think that I could have a copy of the receipts from that night, Ken?"

Ken went and retrieved the copy that Katie had asked for.

"I wouldn't do this for anyone else, Katie, but you were so good to Gram when she was in the hospital that I feel I owe you."

Katie was thinking that being nice does pay off sometimes.

Katie made a purchase of a bottle of white wine and went on her way.

Brenda had touched other bottles of wine in the store. This could explain how her fingerprints had gotten on the bottle of wine found at the murder scene. Could someone be setting her up to take the blame for a murder that she didn't commit? On the other hand, was it just chance that the real murderer had picked up the same bottle that

Brenda had been holding and had left her prints on? Katie was sure that this was what had happened; she would just have to prove it.

Katie stopped under one of the antique streetlights that, like ever-watchful sentinels guarded the beautiful lane to read the receipts that Ken had given to her. The halo of light cast from the streetlight barely illuminated the receipt, but she could still make out what it said. To her surprise she found that there had been only one bottle of red wine, a claret, sold twenty minutes after Brenda had purchased the thirty-dollar bottle of white wine. It turned out that this was the only bottle in that price range that had been sold that evening.

As she walked down the lane, a very eerie feeling overtook her. Katie could have sworn that someone was following her. She could feel the little hairs on her arms and the nap of her neck stand straight up like thousands of little prickly fingers running over her flesh. She was not a skittish person at all, but she definitely knew that there was something wrong. It was like when you are driving down the road and an animal runs out in front of you. First, you get that hot flash of panic surging through the pit of your stomach, then almost as quickly it subsides and is replaced with that icy cold feeling that rushes through your body. Katie increased her stride to almost a trot.

When she finally reached her front porch, she strained her eyes to search the darkness for whatever it was that had frightened her so badly. The gloom of the night was faintly illuminated by the halo of light from the streetlight. She thought that she had glimpsed a shadowy figure ducking into the alley that runs between her house and that of Mrs. Finch, but she could not be sure that her eyes were not playing tricks on her. "Pull yourself together, Katie," she admonished herself. "You're letting your imagination run away with you." She entered the security of her home with her heart still pounding so hard that she could actually hear it. She was almost out of breath as she leaned her back against the solid wooden door. As she stood with her back pressed against the smooth wood of the door, she was desperately trying to calm herself before entering the living room where she instinctively knew George would be. She knew that she had bitten her lower lip, when the coppery taste of blood filled her mouth.

George was sitting in his recliner in the living room. "You look as if you've seen a ghost," he said jokingly.

Katie told him what had just happened.

"I'm calling Joe right now," he said as he jumped up from the chair, his joking manner transformed into one of concern.

"Don't be ridiculous, George. I'm fine and it was probably just my imagination anyway."

"I don't like it, Katie. You never panic about anything. Did you see who it was?"

"No, I tried, but it's much too dark to see down the alley from the front porch."

"Katie, maybe you should give up the amateur detective stuff. It could be very dangerous, you know." George was holding her tightly in his arms by this time, and she felt completely safe in his warm embrace.

That night they were having another ACDC meeting. Katie arrived on time to this one. George had insisted on accompanying her to the entrance of the mansion after what had happened earlier that evening.

"I'm not going to let you take anymore chances, Katie. Sometimes you are too brave for your own good. I will go down to the Fox and Hound and have a couple of beers. I will be back here after the meeting so that I can walk you home." He gave her a kiss and waited for her to enter the front door of the mansion before turning to leave.

As she entered the room, she noticed immediately that Tom Crook still had not rejoined their ranks. This made her feel much more comfortable since he had made it to the top of her suspect list once again.

They went through the regular preamble of the rules of order, while Katie sat there chomping at the bit. She could not wait to divulge her newest findings to the group.

She had a feeling that they shared in her urgency by the looks on their faces.

Katie told everyone what she had learned over the last couple of days.

When she arrived at the part about the phone message, they made her repeat what she had written down four times.

Mr. Thomson immediately asked her, "Katie, are you sure that there's not a pause between the words Jane and better?"

"I'm absolutely positive. I listened to the tape over and over again just to make sure."

"And there were no other words, just what you stated?"

"I'm positive."

"This sounds more as if it is a statement being made to someone else instead of something that one would say on the telephone," Mr. Thomson said.

She said that the same thought had occurred to her.

Katie also told them about Brenda being in the liquor store. She told them how Ken was sure that she had been touching different wine bottles.

"That would explain how her fingerprints came to be on that particular bottle," Mrs. Finch chirped. "Anyone watching her could have picked that bottle of wine up after she left the store, and they could have used it to administer the poison to Ann." She was looking deep in to Katie's eyes as she made this statement.

Colonel Simons had been quiet up until this point. "I have been doing a little investigating on my own. When I heard that Dick Carlson was the prosecutions star witness, I confronted him. He stated emphatically that Brenda had been carrying a bottle in a bag from the liquor store that night. I then asked him if it appeared to be one or two bottles. He said that he was positive that there had been only a single bottle in the bag. If anyone would know the exact size of a single bottle of wine in a paper bag, it would be Dick."

Now they knew for sure that Brenda had purchased only one bottle of wine. They were also sure from what Ken had told Katie that it was a very expensive white wine that Brenda had purchased. Since the only other bottle of wine sold that night had been purchased twenty minutes after Brenda had already left the liquor store, it would only make sense that someone other than Brenda was the one who purchased the wine in which the antifreeze was found.

"I better tell all of you the other thing that Mrs. Finch and I found out." Katie looked her way as she said this, and Mrs. Finch gave her a smile.

"They found one of Ann's rings in Brenda's house. It was in the drawer of an antique dresser that she had in her garage, and the DA is now absolutely positive that she stole the ring after killing Ann."

"Balderdash," Mr. Thomson said. "Anyone could have gone into Brenda's garage and placed the ring there. She never kept the door locked and everyone knows it."

"Yes, I have even gone to her garage to borrow a gardening tool when she wasn't at home," the Colonel said. "Of course I had her permission to do so," he hurriedly added.

"We will all testify in court that anyone could have placed the ring there to try and frame Brenda." None of the people present really cared for Brenda that much, but this was a mystery and they all wanted to solve it.

"Now that you mention it, I saw Tom Crook by Brenda's garage the day after Ann was buried," put in Mrs. Finch. "I thought it was odd, his hanging around like that, but I didn't really think too much about it until now."

She could be making this up, but Katie doubted it very much. Mrs. Finch was not a grandstander, so she was probably telling the truth.

"Another thing I thought very odd was, that when I saw him I could swear that he was smoking a cigarette. I never remember him smoking before so it stuck in my head," Mrs. Finch said. She had a broad smile on her wrinkled little face as she made this statement.

"Joe had mentioned that there were cigarette butts found near the garage when they were searching for evidence at Brenda's house. He even asked me if I knew whether she smoked or not. I told him that she absolutely didn't smoke because her father had died of lung cancer, and she made it very clear to anyone that lit up in front of her that it was a disgusting habit," Katie told them. "Now that I think of it I noticed that he smelled of cigarette smoke at Ann's wake the other night. I never remember seeing him smoke, but I'm sure of what I smelled." Katie looked at the others.

They all sat there pondering these newest revelations. It certainly appeared that the police had jumped to the wrong conclusion.

"Katie, you have to go and tell Chief Joe everything that you have told us. Perhaps we should hold a special meeting, and we can tell him what I have come up with?" Colonel Simons said this without the least bit of embarrassment that he was again attempting to take credit for what the whole group had come up with.

"No, Katie Scarlett will go to Joe and tell him everything that we have come up with." This came from Mrs. Finch. She did not often stand up to the Colonel, but the look on her face said that she would give him a tongue lashing if he again opened his mouth.

As promised, George was waiting for Katie after the meeting. They walked home hand in hand as if they were newlyweds. She felt so safe when she was in her husband's presence, and she was glad that he had insisted on walking her home. She told him what had gone on at the meeting that night.

"Honey, I wish you and the rest of the group would leave this matter up to Joe. He is capable of solving it on his own, don't you think?"

"We are just trying to help him, George. I mean they say two heads are better than one. So look how much help all of our heads will be when you put them together."

The next day Katie once again made her way to Joe's office and told him what the ACDC had discovered.

He looked very interested and promised that he would investigate the matter.

"Katie, this really doesn't prove anything. I mean Brenda's fingerprints are on the wine bottle, and Dick Carlson could be mistaken as to how many bottles of wine were in the bag." This was very hard to believe since Dick could almost tell you what kind of bottle was in the bag just by the outline of the bottle that the bag contained. Everyone knew that he was the liquor store's best customer. It would be very doubtful that he would make a mistake as to the contents of one of the liquor stores bags, since he had seen them so many times.

"What if she had gone home and had another bottle of wine there. She could have substituted it for the expensive wine," Joe said.

"You're grasping for straws, Joe, and you know it. There is no way that Brenda waited around the liquor store for twenty minutes after she bought the first bottle of wine. Ken would have noticed this and told me right away if she had. Remember he said that she rarely came into the store, so he would have noticed this. I also cannot believe that she just so happened to have another bottle of wine at home that she could have used. If she had, she would have served it to her guests when they came over for dinner. After all, she didn't know until Ken told her what kind of wine is usually served with fish." Katie had an almost pleading look as she gazed at Joe.

She then told him what Mrs. Finch had said about Tom being near Brenda's garage.

"There's no law against standing outside of someone's garage, is there?" he said as he tried to change the subject.

"No there isn't, but you told me that there were cigarette butts found outside of the garage, and I know for a fact that Brenda would never smoke."

"Mrs. Finch could be wrong you know. I mean she is getting up there in age and she may have thought that Tom had a cigarette when he didn't."

"She may be eighty, but her eyesight is excellent. You know that she doesn't miss anything that is going on in the neighborhood, Joe."

"That's the truth; she is a pretty dependable witness. I have questioned her in the past about occurrences near her house, and she is very good at giving the most precise details about her surroundings."

"After all," Katie said to him. "At the wake the other night I distinctly smelled cigarette smoke on Tom's clothing, Joe. I have never seen him smoke, but people who don't smoke usually don't reek of tobacco smell."

"I'll check it out, okay, Katie."

"This is a matter of getting the right person behind bars you know."

"I'm well aware of that fact," Joe said in a very somber tone.

Katie told Joe that she had to go and made her departure. She desperately needed him to believe her story. She wanted to get Brenda off these charges. After all, she did feel as if she owed her something, even though she could not explain why she felt this way, even to herself.

That night Katie and George received a phone call from Joe. He had taken the empty bottle, which had been found at the scene of the crime, to the liquor store. They scanned it on the scanner, and the numbers matched those that were on the sales slip. They now knew that the bottle of wine had been used to poison Ann was purchased twenty minutes after Brenda had made her purchase. They knew that she had been long gone from the store by this time.

Joe said, "I don't know how we missed this, but I am having Ken come in tomorrow so that I can question him more thoroughly. This weakens the prosecution's case quite a bit, Katie. I also spoke to Dick, and he is absolutely sure that there was only one bottle of wine in the bag that Brenda was carrying."

"When I questioned Mrs. Finch, she was adamant about Tom being near Brenda's garage. Therefore, I went over to see him, on the pretense, that we may have some new leads in the investigation. While I was there, I looked around for ashtrays or any tell tale signs that he was a smoker. I didn't see anything in or around the house to give me a clue to this, but then I looked at his hands. Sure enough he had the tell tale yellow-orange tobacco stains between his index and middle fingers of his right hand. It's always a dead give away if someone smokes."

"Good job, Joe," Katie said with a great amount of enthusiasm.

"I know that you find it hard to believe, Katie, but I am pretty good at my job you know."

"Well, you're going to let Brenda go then?" she asked trying to change the subject.

"That's up to the prosecutor. He still has a very strong case against her, even though you have weakened it greatly."

"He doesn't have a case at all, and you know it, Joe."

"He is going to be very upset and embarrassed that your group has foiled his perfect case, I can tell you that, Katie."

"Don't you worry about that? We are working on finding the true identity of the murderer, and we will let you know of anything we discover that could help you. I do not think that the prosecutor believes that anyone, other than the police and his office, has the mentality to figure this thing out. We are going to prove him wrong, Joe."

"What about Tom leaving the room?" Katie asked him. "Did you find out if he left at any point during the meeting?" She was still certain that Tom had something to do with his wicked wife's death.

"Yes, he did leave for a brief period, from 9:15 to 9:25. He told the others that he had to take his heart medication."

"They didn't happen to remember the name of the medication, did they?"

"Yes, it was Cardizem. One of the other men took the same thing, and he remembered what it was. I knew, you being a nurse, that you would want to know the name of it."

"You're supposed to take Cardizem before meals and at bedtime," Katie replied. "Why would he take it at such an odd time? I mean he knew how long the meeting was going to last more than likely, so why would he leave just at the time that the phone call was made. This sounds sort of fishy to me."

"I did ask them if he'd said that he'd forgotten it, but they all said he stated that it was time to take it, and he couldn't miss the dose."

This was very odd indeed, Katie thought. The doctor should have told him when to take this drug, and knowing Tom, he would be very careful to follow the doctor and pharmacy recommendations. Katie would keep this in mind, since she felt that it was very important.

"By the way, how can you be positive of the time that he left the room? I mean most people don't sit there and look at their watches constantly."

"One of the men at the meeting took the opportunity to make a phone call to a colleague as soon as Tom left the room. He said that the conversation lasted until Tom returned. When we checked his phone records, it gave the exact time of the call he had made."

"This still doesn't prove anything, Katie. Tom didn't have enough time to go home, make Ann make the call, and then kill her, you know."

"No he didn't. But it sure gives us something to think about, doesn't it?"

Katie thanked Joe for the information and hung up the phone. Her mind was full of the matter at hand.

Her conversation with Joe had certainly given Katie some ideas. If Tom left the room, then he could have been the one to make the phone call to the Hastings house. She just did not know quite yet how this was accomplished, but she certainly was going to try to figure it out.

Katie decided to go to the library to get a mystery that had just made it on the best sellers list. She entered the library, waving at Mrs. Hicks as she made her way to the mystery section. She searched in vain for the mystery, but couldn't remember the name of the book. She went to the computer section in the lowest level to try to obtain the name of the book from the computer. The glow of the computer screens cast elongated shadows on the walls as she made her way to one of the terminals.

All of a sudden, Katie was overtaken with an eerie feeling. She could feel the presence of someone else in the room, but with the dull light it was difficult to tell just who it was that shared the room with her. She could feel her skin prickling, as the tiny hairs on her arms, and nap of her neck stood up. Katie had the uncanny feeling that she was being watched, as though she were a mouse being stealthy stalked by a cat. She shivered, even though the room was not chilly at all.

All of a sudden, there was a voice directly behind her. She whirled around to find the owner of the voice and came face to face with Tom Crook. He looked much older than he had before the death of his wife, and it appeared as if he were under a terrible strain.

Being a nurse, she would have had empathy for anyone else in his condition, but she just couldn't feel sorry for this man, no matter how hard she tried.

"Hello, Tom," Katie stammered out.

He stood there in the dim light not saying a word.

"Did you want to use this computer?" She tried to make her voice sound braver than she was feeling at the moment.

"No, Katie, what I want is for you to drop the investigation of my poor wife's death. I know that you have been questioning people about me, and I want it to cease."

Katie wondered how he knew that she had been questioning anyone. Someone must have told him that she had been asking questions as to his whereabouts on the day of the murder. Well, this was Greenbrier, and everyone knew that it was full of gossips.

"You are nothing but an interfering busy body. I think that you should mind your own business and stay out of the investigation," he said ominously.

"Whatever do you mean?" She asked with a bit more bravado than she actually felt.

"You have been trying to get the murderer of my poor wife out of jail, and you have been questioning every one to my whereabouts around the time of the murder. You certainly can't think that I had anything to do with it, can you? I do have an airtight alibi for the time of her death, you know."

"Oh, I didn't know that the coroner had come up with an exact time of death," she tried to sound as innocent as she could.

"You know very well that the death occurred somewhere between 9:20 and 1:00, and since I was at the office the entire time, no one could think that I had anything to do with it."

"I just want to try to find out the identity of the murderer, Tom. I'm sure that you would like to know, too."

"No." The word came out more like a hiss than she thought he intended. "Not if you are trying to involve me or my children in this awful deed," he continued scowling at her. "We had nothing to do with it. If you persist in this harassment of me and my family I am going to sue you for slander, Katie."

"Are you recording this conversation, Tom, so you can use it in a slander case against me?" she questioned him.

His hand instinctively went to his left breast pocket, and then went back to his side almost as quickly. It was a well-known fact that he carried a small tape recorder at all times, just in case the need arose. Katie looked at the front of his shirt and knew immediately that no recorder was there. There was no tell tale bulge in the pocket as she had noticed in the past. Where was the recorder now, Katie wondered to herself?

He did not answer her question, but instead said. "You know there is a great deal of evidence supporting the fact that the murderer is Brenda. On the other hand, there are many other suspects that I could name. It even could have been your husband, George. He hated my wife because of the lawsuit that he lost against us. Perhaps you should be looking a little closer to home for the murderer?"

"That's ridiculous, Tom. George would never kill anyone and everybody knows it."

"Are you so sure of that?" His eyes had never left hers during the conversation.

"Yes, I'm positive." Katie was looking for a way to end the conversation when old Mrs. Hicks appeared out of nowhere at her side.

Katie jumped at her sudden appearance.

"Mrs. Hicks, I didn't hear you coming," Katie stammered.

"Well, dear, I am a librarian, and you know that I like to keep my library quiet," she said with a look that went from Tom to Katie.

"It's almost closing time. Therefore, I thought I'd better come and see if you were still here. You wouldn't want to be accidentally locked in, Katie."

She then turned her attention to Tom.

"I didn't even see you come in, Tom. So it's a good thing that I checked, isn't it?" She was glaring at Tom as she spoke these words. Katie could see from the look on Mrs. Hicks's face that she knew Katie was extremely uncomfortable.

"Katie, I would like you to wait and walk me home if you would, dear."

She was making it known to Tom that Katie would not be walking home alone. Katie knew that she felt the danger in the same way that she herself did.

"It's very dark out and I would feel much more comfortable if we walked home together after I lock up." She was speaking to Katie, but her eyes never left Tom's face.

"I would be happy to walk home with you," Katie said with much noted relief in her voice.

As they were walking home, Mrs. Hicks startled her by saying. "I don't trust that man at all, Katie. You should keep your distance from him."

"There is something very ominous about him, isn't there?" Katie replied.

"I think that he is out to make trouble for someone," Mrs. Hicks said. "I think that he knows the true identity of the murderer, but that he is trying to throw the blame towards Brenda."

"So you don't think that Brenda did it either?"

"Absolutely not," she said in a tone that left no room for argument. "Brenda may be many things, but a thief is definitely not one of them."

Katie dropped Mrs. Hicks at her front door and then made a beeline home. As she turned to make sure she was not being followed, she could see from the glow of Mrs. Hicks's porch light that she was waiting for Katie to enter the security of her front door. Katie was sure that she was concerned about her safety.

The next afternoon Mrs. Finch went by Katie's house, and Katie let her know about her and Joe's conversation. She then told her about the confrontation at the library. She told her how odd it was that the tape player that was always on Tom's person seemed to be missing.

"This could be a clue, dear. I'm not quite sure what it could mean, but I'm sure that he's up to no good."

"Those are my thoughts exactly."

"Katie Scarlett, you really think that Tom has something to do with this, don't you?" There was a twinkle in her eye.

"I can't get it out of my head that he was the one that would gain the most by his wife's death. We all know that she made his life almost unbearable. After all she hated his children, and she was constantly spending money in a fashion that appeared to be way above their means."

"If we could just figure this thing out it would be wonderful, dear. I just don't know how he could have managed to kill her with so many people saying that he had never left work that day."

"I know, it truly is a mystery that has to be solved. If we don't, someone else that we know will be placed on the top of the police suspect list."

"Who do you think they will go after next? There are so many people that hated that woman, it could be any of us." Mrs. Finch was giving her a searching look as she made this statement.

"Joe really hasn't told me if they have someone else on their list yet. As you said, it could be anyone." Katie was thinking that Mrs. Finch was more than likely on top of Joe's list. After all she did have a very strong motive after what the woman had done to poor little Baby, if Ann indeed had killed him, which was a very good possibility. As she looked at this frail little woman she could not picture her killing anyone, but stranger things have happened.

The next day was Thanksgiving and Katie had invited Mrs. Finch over for dinner. Katie could not bear the thought of anyone being alone during the holidays. Mrs. Finch had no relatives since the death of her husband, and it pulled at Katie's heartstrings to know that she would be alone in her big old house. Mrs. Finch had graciously declined the invitation, saying that her arthritis was acting up. "I will be fine, dear. When you reach my age you will find that you'd rather just stay at home and remember the years gone by."

"Don't forget that I am going to bring your dinner over around two o'clock tomorrow."

"You are such a caring person Katie Scarlett. No wonder you are such a wonderful nurse. I will leave the side entrance through the garage open so you can come in to the kitchen. That way you won't have to walk all the way around to the front entrance."

Thanksgiving Day was always very special to Katie's family and friends. They would gather and give thanks for all that they had. George and Katie would always make an enormous feast with all of the trimmings.

Not having any immediate family in the area, Joe was always invited to join them. Their children were also present, and it was wonderful to have them home. Her sons were tall and handsome beyond belief. They, fortunately, had both been blessed with their father's good looks. Rachel, who resembled Katie, was walking on air since her boyfriend Tony accompanied her. He seemed very likeable, and Katie was happy Rachel had found someone she truly seemed to adore.

Terrie, Katie's friend from work was also present. She had decided it was too long a trip for her to go home for just one day. She would have to turn right around and return to work by the following morning. Therefore, she happily accepted Katie's offer to spend the day with her and her family. Terrie had long blonde hair that fell in ringlets over her shoulders. Her eyes were the bluest blue that Katie had ever seen. They appeared especially bright today.

Katie, as she had promised, prepared a huge platter of turkey and stuffing with all of the trimmings to take over to Mrs. Finch. She told the rest of the group that she would be right back after she delivered the meal.

As she made her way through Mrs. Finch's garage, she noticed as she always had, that nothing had been touched since the death of Mrs. Finch's husband fourteen years before. All of his tools were in perfect alignment on the workbench, just as he had left them. The garage floor was as neat as a pin even after all of these years. It appeared to be the same as it always had. It was the same as on the day Katie had entered it to see if there were anything that poor little Baby could have gotten in to when he had become so ill. Nothing had changed with the exception of one thing. It caught her eye immediately, and her stomach knotted up almost making her sick. There on the shelf on the wall was a gallon size yellow jug. She knew what it was immediately without having to read the front of it. It was antifreeze. She knew that it had not been there when she had previously examined the garage.

Katie's mind was racing in many directions. Why would Mrs. Finch have purchased antifreeze? There was absolutely no reason for her to do this that Katie could think of. The car that her and her husband had owned was a VW bug, so even if she had decided to start to drive it again she would not need antifreeze for it.

Katie entered Mrs. Finch's kitchen with her thoughts racing. Should she ask her why she had bought antifreeze? It would sound as if she were accusing her of something if she did no matter how she tried to broach the subject, Katie thought. On the other hand, she did not think that she could go back to her house and act as if she had not seen what she had. She was not good at hiding things, and she knew that everyone would know that something was up. God, why had Mrs. Finch not gotten rid of the evidence before someone saw it. She knew that Katie never missed too much that was going on around her. Did she want her to know what she had done? Katie was so sick inside by the time that she entered Mrs. Finch's kitchen that she could barely speak.

"Katie Scarlett, that smells wonderful," Mrs. Finch said as she came from the dining room entranceway. "You are the best neighbor that anyone could ever have, dear. I feel so lucky to have you as a friend."

A friend. That is what Katie was to this poor frail old woman. She could not stand the thought of Mrs. Finch being locked away for the rest of her life in jail. She would not even be able to live through a trial, let alone be locked up in a tiny cell. Perhaps she was jumping to the wrong conclusion, Katie thought. She would not say anything about this just yet. Katie could not be the one that was responsible for taking what little time she had left on this earth.

"I hope that you enjoy your dinner," Katie stammered not able to look Mrs. Finch in the eye.

"Katie Scarlett, are you feeling unwell? You look a little green around the gills," Mrs. Finch said in her singsong little voice.

"I think that it's all of the excitement. You know having all of the family home and worrying that the dinner won't be perfect."

"Yes I remember how it was when I was young, and my mother-in-law would come for a meal. You always think that something will go dreadfully wrong."

"That is exactly the way I am feeling right now," Katie said to her. "If you need anything please call over to the house, and I will be right over."

"Thank you so much, dear. Have a wonderful visit with your family."

As she left the house, Katie thought that if she could hide this secret from her family she would be one of the best actors of all time. She would have to make up some excuse so that if they detected a change in her mood she would have a story prepared.

No one seemed to notice that anything was wrong when Katie rejoined her family. They all talked about what was going on in their lives and the changes that had happened since their last get together.

As they sat down to the huge turkey dinner, Rachel brought up the conversation about the murder. "So how goes the murder in Hooterville, mom?"

Rachel had moved to the city to attend college. Even though she loved the little village of Greenbrier, she often referred to it at Hooterville, the small community on the TV show "Green Acres," which she had watched reruns of as a child.

Joe was the first one to speak. "Your mother threw a monkey wrench into my investigation with her sleuthing, I can tell you that. I had what I'd call an airtight case, and she and her cronies made me and the DA's office look rather foolish." He was looking dead at Katie when he said this.

"You wouldn't want to have the wrong person in jail for a crime that they didn't commit, would you?" Rachel was busily making little rivers of gravy run down the hill of mashed potatoes that Katie had given her. She was never as big an eater as her brothers were, and did more playing with her food than eating it.

"No, I wouldn't, but at least she could have given me another suspect to replace Brenda with," Joe replied.

George was also looking at Katie as if he could read her thoughts. If anyone would notice a change in her after she had returned from Mrs. Finch's home, it would be her loving husband.

"Oh, don't worry Uncle Joe." The children had always called him "Uncle Joe," even though there were no family ties to him. "From what Mom says she hasn't given up investigating this case yet, not by a long shot." This statement came from her eldest son, Jay. Jay was giving Joe the mischievous little grin that always warmed Katie's heart.

Joe, her middle child, spoke up. "If anyone can solve a mystery, it would be good old mom, the amateur sleuth. She always knows the murderer in movies before anyone else does," he said with a great deal of pride in his voice. That is if she doesn't fall asleep. He did not mean this as a cut to Uncle Joe Katie was sure, but it came out that way. Joe, on the other hand, seemed oblivious to everything that was going on around him, with the exception of Terrie, which Katie was quite thankful for at this moment.

Good Old George sat there with that I told you so look on his face directed at Chief Joe.

Joe was being so attentive towards Terrie that he totally missed the look.

Was there something going on here, Katie wondered. Wouldn't it be great if Terrie and Joe got together? They would make a stunning couple. He was so dark and handsome, and she was so blonde and fair. Katie would have to work on this. After all Terrie had been divorced for two years now, and Joe was an eligible bachelor. Katie was already picturing the wedding.

After everyone had eaten their fill her sons having devoured everything in sight, the women got up to clean the table.

As they did the dishes Rachel said, "Mom, I can't believe that you got that old battle-axe of a Brenda Cormick off the charges. What were you thinking? She has been so mean towards you for so many years because you snatched dad away from her that you should have left her to be found guilty. At least that way you wouldn't have had her as an enemy anymore."

"Haven't you heard, Rachel? Your mom and Brenda are now on very friendly terms. After your mom weakened the DA's case so much with her sleuthing, they felt they no longer could hold Brenda for the murder and they let her out on her own recognizance. Your mom then went to the jail and picked her up," Terrie put in.

This indeed was true. Ever since Katie had proven that Brenda had more than likely not murdered Ann, or in any case, that she was not as good a suspect as the police had thought, Brenda had reformed. She would even stop in and visit Katie now and then. Moreover, it appeared that she no longer hated her. In fact, they were becoming quite friendly indeed.

Terrie went on. "She even brings your mom homemade jams and jellies to work, and they go off to a corner table and chat."

"You don't eat anything that she brings you, do you mom? I mean the woman was accused of poisoning someone you know."

"Don't worry, Rachel," Katie said. "I always wait until she tastes the food first," Katie said with a laugh. "She still may be after your dad, and what better opportunity for her to get him than my being out of the way." They all laughed at this.

"You still better be careful, mom. No one would expect her to try to poison anyone, not after she had already been accused of doing just that. She could bump you off, and no one would be the wiser," Rachel said as she began to put the leftovers away.

The kids were staying at the house with George and Katie for a few more nights. They were all happy that Katie had kept their rooms just the way that they had left them. Of course, Tony had the couch to sleep on, since George and Katie thought that this was only proper.

After they all promised to get together again over the Christmas holidays, Joe and Terrie decided to make their departures. Joe said he would walk Terrie to her car as he helped her on with her coat. Was this love blossoming? Katie would question Terrie very thoroughly the next time they worked together. As they were leaving, Terrie and Joe thanked them for having them and said it was the best turkey they'd ever had. This statement was made every year after one of Katie and George's wonderful family feasts. George had really out done himself this year. He had tried a new recipe and had used the deep fat fryer to cook the turkey this year. It had turned out perfectly.

Life was good, Katie thought. If she only had not seen what she had in Mrs. Finch's garage.

George and Katie always went out for a long stroll after a big meal. The air was brisk and had turned very chilly.

"What's up Katie?" he asked her. He was giving her a very intent look.

"What do you mean?" she almost blurted.

"I noticed it as soon as you returned from Mrs. Finch's house. You were fine when you left, but you seemed almost nervous when you got back. Was she ill or something?"

"No, she isn't ill or anything. In fact, she is doing better than she has in years. It is just that you know how I hate to see someone alone on a holiday. I often wonder what I would do if I didn't have all of you here with me."

"Don't worry, sweetheart. It will be a very long time before you are without me by your side, and you will always have the kids." He placed his strong arm around her waist as he always did when they were out for a walk. It was a very comforting feeling for Katie.

She felt like such a liar, but she just couldn't tell George what she had discovered, not just yet anyway.

Katie had a very restless sleep that night. She had dreams of Mrs. Finch sitting in a courtroom, while the judge, wearing a long black robe, slammed his gavel down uttering the words, "you have been found guilty of the murder of Ann Crook. You are sentenced to spend the remainder of your natural life in prison."

The next morning as the whole family, including Tony, sat down to a huge breakfast George had cooked, the murder was once again the main topic of discussion.

"Who is your prime suspect now, Mom?" This question came from Jay.

"I really don't know, there are so many possibilities. Mrs. Finch could be a suspect; she probably has the best motive." God she did not know why she had said this. She looked around to see if anyone had noticed anything wrong. Everyone knew the story about her little dog, but they did not know what Katie had found in her garage. Katie hurriedly went on. "You have Mr. Thomson and the Colonel, who run neck and neck for a spot on my suspect list. Your dad could also be a contender for a place on the list, because of the trouble that those two people have caused him. But if I had to name who I really thought that it was, it would be Tom, Ann's husband."

Jay said he thought that Tom had an airtight alibi. He made this observation as he spread homemade jelly onto his fourth piece of toast.

Katie said, "That is what the police think. But you know, something keeps nagging me about the phone call that Ann made to the Hastings."

Joe was filling his plate for the second or third time, Katie had lost track. "If mom thinks that she knows the identity of the murderer, she is more than likely correct. I mean, we know from experience that not much gets past her," Joe said as he began to eat once again.

"I just wish that I knew more about cell phones," Katie said.

Rachel became quite excited at this. "Tony is an expert on cell phones, mom." She gave him an adoring look and he blushed. "He works for a cell phone company on his summers off."

Katie asked Tony if there was anyway to tell where the phone call had been made from.

"If there is only one tower for service in town, the call would have been routed through that tower. However, they would not be able to tell exactly where the call was made from," he added as he began to eat his breakfast.

There was only one tower in town, of this Katie was sure. It stood on the tallest mountain in the area and she often thought that if the light in it ever went out that a plane could easily hit it.

George asked if the call could have been forwarded through her cell phone from another phone in any way. Tony went into detail as to how this could have been done, but Katie did not see Tom being able to figure this out.

As they sat there eating the wonderful breakfast George had prepared for them, it just so happened that a cell phone rang. Katie noticed that all of the kids immediately reached for their cell phones with the exception of Tony. They discovered that it was Jay's phone that was ringing, and he excused himself to take the call.

"Tony, I noticed that when the phone rang everyone checked to see if it was theirs except for you, why didn't you have to check?" Katie asked.

"I have a special ring tone programmed into my phone. This way I can tell immediately if its mine that's ringing, or if it is someone else's."

"What do you mean?" She sat there not knowing what he was talking about.

"Rach, go in the other room and call my number," he told Rachel.

She obediently went into the other room and made the call.

The phone did not ring but played a country music tune. Tony picked up and told Rachel to return to the dining room.

"It's the newest thing, Mrs. Adams. Instead of your phone just ringing, you can have any kind of tune you want programmed into your phone. It makes it much easier to know if it is your phone ringing or someone else's.

Katie found this quite interesting. She really did not know why, but it intrigued her nonetheless.

Rachel and Katie left the mess for the men to clean up. It was, after all, Black Friday, and they wanted to get to the stores before all of the best sales were over.

They had a very pleasant conversation while they walked to town, and Rachel said that she felt Tony was going to be getting her an engagement ring very soon. Katie was happy for her. Her little peanut, as she had called her when she was little, was now a gorgeous young woman. She would make a great wife and mother, Katie thought with pride.

As they walked down the lane Rachel keeping right up to Katie's long strides, she said. "You really don't think that dad killed that woman, do you, mom?" Katie could hear the concern in her voice.

"Absolutely not, Rachel. Your dad is one of the kindest and gentlest men I have ever known."

"Well, it would be rather fun for you to figure out a way that he could have done it you know." Katie could see the mischievous little smile that crossed Rachel's face as she said this.

"Rachel, wherever did you get your quirky sense of humor from?"

"I believe dad said that I got it from you," was her reply.

"As my mom use to say, the nut doesn't fall far from the tree. I guess you are a great deal more like me than I had noticed." In fact, as she gazed at her gorgeous daughter she could see herself as a young woman looking back at her.

They finally reached their destination, which was a small boutique that Rachel and she always shopped at. They stood there trying to decide on the best shopping tactic to use: should they stay together or go their separate ways so that they could find the best bargains? As they were being pushed and pulled along with the throng of other shoppers, Katie noticed Kay ahead of them. She only knew her as Kay, since she resided in Simmons, but Katie knew that she was Tom Crook's secretary. She approached her and asked if she was having any luck finding any good sales. Kay also knew Katie by sight and said that she had found some really good bargains. Katie then changed the topic of discussion and asked her how Tom was doing.

"Oh, he hasn't been into work except for one time since the murder."

"It must be very difficult on him," was Katie's reply.

"I guess it would be difficult to have your wife murdered. I mean most people would find it so. Who would ever think that such a thing could happen, in such a small village as Greenbrier?" Katie could hear in her voice that she really didn't seem to think that it was going to be a great hardship on Tom.

"Do you think that he's going to be okay?" Katie asked her as they stood amongst the many shoppers.

"Well, frankly, I can't see where he's going to miss her that much. After all, he always put on a good front. He always called her his lovely wife and would act as if nothing was wrong." Kay gave her a knowing look. "But I overheard them on many occasions when they thought that they were alone, and I don't think they really cared that much for one another."

"So you had heard them arguing?" Katie persisted.

"Not so much arguing. It was more as if he were just fed up with her. Not only her, but also everything about her. None of us at work ever liked him much, and when she came in, he would be even more overbearing than he normally was. I think that he knew she was just with him for his money, but was afraid to divorce her because she was so vindictive."

Katie went on with her questions even though the crowd was pushing them along as they spoke.

"Did you notice if Tom left his office that day, even for a short time?"

"The police have already asked me that, Katie. I am absolutely positive that he did not leave. He did go to his office to take a medicine that he said he had forgotten to take that morning." She had a rather unusual look on her face when she said this. "You know I can't remember him ever taking any pills while at work. I didn't even know that he had a medical problem."

"Did you notice anything else unusual that day?"

"What do you mean by unusual?"

"You know, did he say anything that was out of the ordinary? Or did he make or take any phone calls that were unusual?"

"Yes, I did notice something odd now that you ask. As Tom was walking past my desk I heard what sounded to me like a bit of classical music being played. It wasn't like an actual piece of music, it was more like the ring tone from a cell phone that everyone uses these days. This is what made me notice him. I was rather busy that day and when I heard the music, I looked up. This was when he told me that he had to take his pill."

Did everyone know about these ring tones except her, Katie wondered.

"Why did you think this odd?" Katie asked.

"Tom's phone, which I had heard many times, always just rang like any other cell phone. I even thought to myself that Mr. Big Shot must think that this will impress us. I mean he doesn't even like classical music. He had complained on many occasions that this was the only kind of music that his wife liked, and he couldn't stand it. Actually, he didn't like music at all. We weren't even permitted to play Christmas music like everyone else does when the holidays are here."

"Did he answer the phone?" Katie persisted.

She thought about this for a moment. "No as a matter of fact he didn't. He just mumbled that he had to take his pill and kept on walking like he didn't even hear the music playing."

Katie had another question. "On the day that he came in to the office after Ann's death, did he work or was he there for some other reason?"

"He said that he had to get something from his desk. That was the day that the chief of police came in to talk to him."

"Did he retrieve whatever it was from his desk?" Katie questioned her.

"I doubt if he would have had time. As he was walking into his office, the chief showed up, and I'm pretty sure that Tom walked back out to where my desk is to talk to him. As a matter of fact he didn't because I remember that they walked out of the building together."

"Could someone come to the office, say in the middle of the night, and not be seen?" Katie went on.

"There is no way that this could have happened. We have security cameras and a guard is constantly at the front desk so you have to sign in if you come in after hours."

Katie wished Kay happy holidays and they separated.

She now had the pieces of the puzzle that had for so long eluded her. If Tom had exchanged cell phones with Ann before he left for work that morning, he could have placed the call from her phone when he went into his office. Katie was sure that it was her phone that he had that day. Kay had said that she had heard the ring tone, and Katie was sure that she was telling the truth. He could have killed her before leaving for work. The hot water in the hot tub would have made it very difficult for the coroner to pin down the exact time of death. She was sure that he had made a recording of Ann's voice and used it to make the call. It was a well-known fact that he always carried a pocket size tape recorder with him. "You never know when it will come in handy to have a tape recorder, just in case someone makes a statement that later you may want to sue them for slander with." He had made this statement on many occasions. That was the only logical solution as to how it could have been her voice on the Hastings' answering machine. This could be the only way that it could have happened to Katie's way of thinking. That is the reason that Ann had sounded as if she were making a statement instead of an actual phone call. Tom could have taped her making the statement earlier and then played it when he called the Hastings. Ann's phone had been found at the bottom of the hot tub, and was smashed so badly that no one would have been able to check if it was actually hers and not someone else's.

Katie could not believe that for the second time in her life, by shear chance, she had discovered the truth in such a serendipitous way. First she had solved, or at least had convinced everyone, how O.J.'s glove could have ended up where it was found. It had been because her dog had frightened her in the same way that Kato had been frightened by the thumps on his wall. Now just by chance that very morning they had been discussing ring tones, and then by chance Tom's secretary had told her about his phone playing the classical piece of music.

As Katie's father in-law had always said, "I rather be a lucky hunter than a good one any day Katie." Well, Katie would rather be a lucky sleuth than a good one anytime, and she sure was having her share of luck.

Katie went and found Rachel in the crowded store. "We have to leave," she said.

"What's the matter, mom: Didn't you find what you were looking for?"

"I sure did, Rachel," she paused for just a second. "I found exactly what I was looking for. I found a murderer."

Katie explained the whole story on their short walk to the police station. Rachel was so excited she forgot to be mad at Katie for making her leave the stores.

"Mom, you have really done it. Let's go and tell Uncle Joe right away."

They made their way to police headquarters. Katie could not wait to see Joe's face when she told him what she had discovered.

When they walked into Joe's office, he saw the look on their faces.

"This isn't a social call from my two best girls, is it?"

"No, we came to tell you how mom found the real killer, Uncle Joe," Rachel blurted out with the enthusiasm of her youth.

"Oh, God, don't tell me that we have another arm chair detective in the making," he said with a sigh. "Isn't one detective in the family enough for the two of you?"

"I didn't really do anything, Uncle Joe; I'm just here for the ride," Rachel said in her perky little voice as she plopped down in one of the armchairs that faced his desk.

They sat at Joe's desk for the next half hour as Katie told him of her suspicions. He did not say anything until she had completed her scenario and then he said. "Katie, I adore you. I should have married you instead of letting George be the lucky one. What a team we would have made."

"Now if he didn't get rid of the recording, which I think, he hasn't really had a chance to, do, we will have the evidence that we need to make an arrest. Katie, one thing, when I arrest Tom for this murder you're not going to come back and attempt to find him innocent, are you?"

"No, I am completely convinced that he is your murderer. Case closed."

When Rachel and Katie returned home, she called Mr. Thomson and told him some of the details she had found out. He said he would call an emergency meeting of the ACDC. It was going to be held that very night at the Greenbrier Mansion.

Katie entered the library of Greenbrier mansion that evening knowing that she had once again solved a mystery that had been up until this point unsolved. She told them the story as it had played out, and for the second time she saw this group completely awe struck by what she had to say.

Mr. Thomson proclaimed that she had always been his favorite student. "You know, Katie, you always were above average in intelligence. I was lucky to have such a good student. It made my teaching career complete having a student like you."

Colonel Simons said that he knew they would crack the case. "I mean after all we did do it together." Within the week, he would be taking complete credit for solving the murder. Oh well, let him, Katie thought.

Mrs. Finch twittered and chirped, "Katie Scarlett, you have done this town a great favor. I was getting a bit worried that I would be the next suspect on the police list. I know that none of you think me capable of murder, but I had actually thought about bumping Ann off. I wonder if I had whether you could have caught me, Katie Scarlett."

Katie would never tell her how close she had come to making her the prime suspect.

Brenda sat there looking at Katie. Tears filled her eyes and then overflowed down her cheeks. All she could do was mouth the words thank you. Katie went over and hugged her.

The day after Joe arrested Tom, Greenbrier was abuzz with the news. The girls at the Curl Up and Dye treated Katie as if she were a celebrity when she went in for her weekly hair appointment.

Joni glided over to her and gave her a big hug.

"I guess that my question has been answered."

Katie had a puzzled look on her face as Joni went on to explain.

"Remember the day that you were leaving the shop. I had asked you if there was ever a real murder in Greenbrier if you could solve it. Well, I guess my question has been answered." She gave her another hug.

After Katie's hair appointment, she decided to stop in Dixie's for a cup of coffee. The parking lot was filled to overflowing and she was certain that the word of Tom's arrest had more than likely spread like a wildfire. After all, you couldn't keep a secret like this in the little village. As she entered the diner with Mrs. Finch, who Katie had run in to outside, she once again received a standing ovation.

"I hear that they're going to name a drink after you over at the Fox and Hound," the Colonel said. "Of course, I suggested it," he stated matter-of-factly.

Just then, the door opened and in walked Joe with Terrie on his arm. Another case solved it would seem. They immediately came up to her, and Joe told her that he had indeed arrested Tom for the murder of his wife.

The news passed from mouth to ear like a chain reaction. Everyone wanted to hear the whole story, and Joe, said that it would be forthcoming.

Mr. Thomson said, "Joe, when you have all of the information we will hold a special meeting at the Greenbrier Mansion, and everyone is invited to attend." This excited the crowd very much. Not only would they hear the whole truth about the case, but they would also be permitted to be in on one of the ACDC meetings.

Two weeks before Christmas, Joe felt he had learned everything he could from Tom and from doing a thorough investigation.

Katie had been packing all day long Good Old George having decided that they needed to get away for a while, and since Katie had plenty of vacation time, he was giving her a cruise for Christmas.

George came home after work, and after they had eaten supper, they made their way to the Greenbrier estate to join the rest of the village.

Everyone in the village was there guessing by the countless footprints in the newly fallen snow. Huge flakes were drifting down from the heavens as if the angels were having a gigantic pillow fight. The flakes were so large that Katie and George were covered with snow by the time they entered the mansion. Greenbrier Mansion had been turned into a winter wonderland. The statues that adorned the entranceway appeared as if they were wearing cloaks of white velvet. It really was breathtaking to behold.

Joe approached them when they entered the great room.

"Katie, I want you by my side so that you can answer any questions I don't have the answer to." He was smiling at her in a way that only Joe could smile.

"Joe, I'm sure that you would be much better at this than I would," Katie stammered.

"Listen, little sleuth, you are the one that solved this case, and everyone expects you to be up there with me."

Katie followed Joe up to the front of the room dragging Good Old George with her for support.

Joe started with the night of the arrest. "When I went to the Crook's home it was almost as if Tom knew I'd be coming. At first, he sat there quietly, not saying anything. As I questioned him, he finally broke down and admitted the whole thing. It was as if the dam had finally broken, and he seemed almost relieved to be telling me his story. This is the way the story was told."

"He just couldn't stand it anymore. That woman drove him crazy. He was supposed to have retired three years ago, but because of her spending habits, he just could not quit working. Not only that, but he also said that she was such a vindictive bitch, that he could not stand even looking at her anymore. She was so spiteful towards his daughters, and for that matter everyone else that she came in contact with, that he felt that he had to do something."

"It seems he had been planning the murder for several months. He knew everyone hated Ann so much that there would be any number of suspects for me to choose from. He felt sure that Mrs. Finch would be number one on the list. After all Ann had poisoned her little dog, he said, by enticing it onto their property with dog treats. She had won the dog's friendship in this way and then one night she deliberately put hamburger out that was laced with antifreeze. She had been watching a TV show and apparently had learned that many pets died every year from antifreeze poisoning. He couldn't believe it when she actually boasted that she had done this."

All eyes went to Mrs. Finch when this statement was made. Tears were streaming down her little wrinkled face, and everyone in the room looked as if they would join her.

"Ann had told Tom that everyone would figure the dog had gotten into the antifreeze on Mrs. Finch's property. Being relatively new to the area she would not have known that the Finch's had owned a VW Bug, which was something that our own little sleuth Katie had pointed out to me." He gave her a smile as he said this. "She would not have known this since Mrs. Finch never drove, and Mr. Finch had died years before their arrival to Greenbrier. Even if she had known what kind of car they drove, she probably would not have known that a VW doesn't have a radiator, so there would be no need for antifreeze. On the other hand, Tom told me, she probably didn't really care if anyone knew that she had done this terrible deed."

Once again, all eyes turned towards Mrs. Finch. Tears continued running down her little wrinkled face and her frail little body was trembling with her sobbing. Katie went over and put her arm around her shoulders.

Joe continued with his story with a catch in his voice. "He told me that is where he had gotten the idea of how to poison Ann. He had even gone to the great lengths to sneak into Mrs. Finch's garage one night after the murder to place a jug of antifreeze there. He said that he had thought that Katie had seen him because he had followed her from the village. He was even thinking of harming Katie in some way once he knew that she was on his trail. He had another idea that would throw suspicion on George if all else failed, so that our little sleuth would drop the whole idea of finding the killer. He was trying to throw suspicion in a couple of different directions he told me. He knew that so many people hated Ann he was sure I would have my hands full trying to figure out who really did it."

"So that was how the antifreeze got into Mrs. Finches garage," Katie said. "I wondered how it had gotten there." Katie was so glad that for once, she had shut her big mouth and not accused Mrs. Finch of the murder at the time, but now she had let the cat out of the bag.

"You mean that you knew about the antifreeze we found in Mrs. Finch's garage, and you never said anything?" Joe asked as he eyed her.

His look made Katie very nervous. "Well, I knew that Mrs. Finch didn't do it," she said, as she continued to sooth the old woman.

As she looked up at her, Mrs. Finch gave her a grateful look.

Joe took a long moment and then continued with his account of the story. Katie could tell that he was wondering how many other clues she had hidden from him, just to protect this woman that she loved.

"He said that after he had planned the murder. He went to the liquor store on many different occasions, and waited until it was very busy, so that he was not particularly noticed. He had seen Brenda picking up different bottles of wine he told me, so when she had left the store he had chosen a bottle that he was sure would have her fingerprints on it. He was wearing gloves and no one noticed, since it was very cold out, that he hadn't removed them on entering the store. He said that he didn't have time to wait for Mrs. Finch to come in to buy something. When opportunity knocks, answer the door. He said that he was sure Brenda would make just as likely a candidate for the murder, since they had bought the old Victorian right out from under her. He told me that Ann had connections with the realtor and that she had forced her to take their deal and drop Brenda's. Since she had then bragged to Brenda and everyone else about this, he figured that this was a good enough motive."

Brenda sat there nodding her head in confirmation of this.

Joe went on. "He then told me, that after giving her the wine laced with antifreeze, he made sure she was dead by holding her head under the water. He figured the police might do an autopsy with it appearing to be an accidental drowning because Ann was not under a doctor's care. He wanted the blame placed on Brenda for the murder so that all suspicion would be taken away from him."

Joe looked towards Brenda as he said this. She was sitting there with a smile on her face. The smile, which had been missing for so many years, transformed her completely. She no longer looked like the old spinster that everyone had come to know. Now she actually looked quite pretty.

Joe went on. "He knew that the meter reader would more than likely notice Ann's body floating in the hot tub on his way past the sunroom that afternoon, since he read the meter at approximately the same time every month. He thought that it would be hours after the apparent drowning before the body would be discovered. He also knew that it would be difficult to determine a time of death, because the water in the hot tub would keep her body temperature elevated."

"He had another plan if this one failed and he wasn't summoned home. He was going to call Mr. Thomson and ask him if he could go over and check on Ann to see if anything was wrong, because he could not get her on the phone. He had to have the body discovered by someone other than himself so that his alibi would check out. Everyone would figure that she was still alive after he went to work because of the phone call that was made to the Hastings' home. We also knew that he hadn't left his office so he would be cleared, just as he had been."

Everyone looked at Joe as he said this since he had been taken in by it.

Joe went on with his story. "He told me that part way through the meeting, he went to his office on the pretense of taking a medication. This was one of the clues that Katie had noticed immediately. Being a nurse, she knew that it was the wrong time to take this particular medication. A man as picky as Tom was not likely to forget something this important. As a matter of fact, Katie found out that the secretary didn't even know that he was on medication, so it was obvious to our little sleuth that he rarely if ever took it at work. It could have been a coincidence of course, but during a murder investigation, we all know that it isn't good to have too many things out of the ordinary happen. People notice things like this." He gave Katie an appreciative look as he said this.

They were hanging on every word. "Once he was safely inside his office he made the phone call. He said that he had recorded Ann while she was on one of her many tirades about the neighborhood kids. As I said, he had been planning this murder for months. He said that he had recorded conversations that they had, and thought that this would be the perfect one to use." Joe looked around at his audience everyone by this time was at the edge of their chairs.

"He said that after he made the phone call, he had placed the tape recorder in his desk drawer so that he could retrieve it later and erase the tape. Unfortunately for him, but very fortunate for us, he never had a chance to return to his office to do this. When we called him from his home to tell him about the accident, his secretary Kay had taken the call at her desk. He thought that it would have seemed odd for him to go to his office for any reason when he had been summoned home for an emergency. He then told us the one time he attempted to retrieve the tape recorder, so he could delete the message, I arrived, and he decided that he would just wait until everything calmed down before he tried again. Kay told Katie that he had only returned to the office once after the murder, and this was where we got lucky. He never had the opportunity to get rid of the evidence."

"He knew he had to be seen constantly from the time that he had arrived at his office until he was summoned home that day, so he never had a chance to return to his office to retrieve the tape recorder. His house was only a couple of minutes away from his office so he knew that if he was out of site for even a few minutes it may be noticed. After Katie told me her theory, I got a search warrant and went to his office. I found the tape recorder and listened to the tape. Of course, you all know by now what I heard when I played it. It was the identical message that had been left on the Hastings answering machine the morning of the murder."

"He told me he knew that Jane took her youngest child to school everyday at the same time." Everyone's attention was drawn to the Hastings when this statement was made. "That is why he had to make the phone call at exactly this time. He knew that she would not be at home, and that her answering machine would pick up. He could always hang up if someone answered the phone, he told me. He played the tape that he had made for the answering machine. It said, "Jane better keep those damn brats off of our property. Or the police will be called and there will be charges made." He then hung up. This was the reason that Ann had not announced who she was, as one would expect her to do, since it was not really Ann calling Jane. He said that he had not even noticed that there was not a pause or a word between *Jane* and *better*. Unfortunately, for him, Katie and her cronies noticed this right off. We at the police station had thought that she may have been drunk, or that the poison may have already been doing its dirty little deed when we listened to the tape." All of the members of the ACDC smiled as he said this.

"After he had made the phone call from his office, he went back to the meeting and then made his presence known in the office until he received the call from us. He figured that later, everyone who was questioned could say for a fact that he was there until the phone call from the police came in. He could also prove later that he was never without a witness to his whereabouts for the entire time. It appeared as if he had an airtight alibi for the time of the murder."

"You all know the rest of the story. Katie saved all of us a great many headaches. She is the one that truly solved this case, with much appreciation from all of us at the station." As he ended his narrative, he said that Katie would now answer questions.

The first question came from Jane Hasting.

"Katie, why do you suppose that Tom didn't answer the phone while he was walking past Kay's desk? Didn't his not answering it make her more suspicious, than if he would have answered it right away?"

"He couldn't really answer the phone. Since it was Ann's phone that he had to make the call on, so it had to be her phone that he had. The caller would have been expecting Ann to answer the phone. If Tom had answered the caller may have thought about it later, after the murder, and may have told the police about it," Katie said.

"What happened to his phone?" was the next question from the audience. Joe fielded this one. "When we discovered the body, there was indeed a cell phone at the bottom of the hot tub. Of course, we had no reason to think it wasn't Ann's. It had appeared to have been broken somehow, and we assumed that it had happened when she had fallen. Or it could have been that she had been so angry about the Hastings children that she had smashed it on the side of the hot tub in a fit of rage."

"We all know what kind of temper the woman had when she was sober. How mad could she get when she was intoxicated, we had no idea. Tom told us that he had to make sure that we could not check to see if it really was Ann's phone, so he smashed it after killing her. He then threw it in the hot tub to be found by us later. Since his phone was identical to hers, he figured that there would be no question as to the ownership of the phone. That was until Katie found out about the different ring tones, of course."

Someone asked Katie how she had discovered that the phone played a classical tune. She explained what had happened at the breakfast table the morning that she had made up her mind that Tom was the killer. Katie told them that she had no idea about the ring tones until Tony did not answer his phone because he knew that it could not be his from the tone. "When Kay mentioned that the cell phone Tom had that day played a classical piece, and that Tom had expressed his dislike for classical music in the past, I had known that it wasn't his phone that he had that day, but more than likely Ann's, since everyone knew that she liked classical music. Since the phone call to the Hastings was definitely made from Ann's cell phone that morning, the only one that could have made the call was the one that had her phone that day, which of course was Tom. Therefore he had to be the murderer."

"What about the diamond ring being found in Brenda's garage?" This question came from Joni, the beautician.

Joe answered this. "Tom wanted to point the finger of blame on Brenda. Since he had used the wine bottle that she had touched in the store to administer the poison, he wanted to make it seem that she had a reason to kill his wife other than their obvious dislike of one another. He planted the ring in Brenda's garage knowing that we would search her home. He wanted the murder to appear as if the motive had been robbery."

"Joe, why didn't Tom just drowned Ann, instead of going through all of the trouble of poisoning her with the antifreeze?" Mr. Thomson questioned him.

"As I said, Tom knew if Ann had been drowned, he would more than likely be the only suspect. Knowing that most people have a bottle of antifreeze somewhere in their home, he wanted to throw suspicion in all different directions."

"Couldn't, Ann, taste the antifreeze in the wine?"

"That had me baffled too. The coroner, had said, not only should the wine have a sweet taste, but it also would have had a thicker consistency. Once again, Katie came to my rescue. I'd told her, that during the autopsy; they had found Ann had had a head injury in the past, some kind of cranial nerve damage. Katie mentioned to me that if a certain nerve is damaged it can cause you to lose the sense of taste and texture."

Joe looked at Katie.

"The trigiminal nerve," Katie said.

"To my knowledge, Ann had never mentioned a head injury to anyone. It would make sense that the only one who would know about it was Tom. When I questioned him about it, he told me that he had done a great deal of research at the library and he had decided to use antifreeze, since it would be certain to be found during the autopsy. He knew it would take a great deal of time for her to die from the antifreeze, this was the reason he held her head under the water. He wanted someone else blamed for the murder other than him. He used antifreeze so I would have a multitude of other suspects on my list."

There were several more questions, but nothing that Joe and Katie could not handle. When they were finished speaking Katie once again received a standing ovation. Everyone came up to her and congratulated her for a job well done.

Mrs. Finch said, "Katie Scarlett, first solving the Simpson case and then the Greenbrier murder, I hope that you are out of town if I ever decide to murder anyone." Everyone laughed at this statement from such a frail little woman.

As everyone stood around discussing the outcome of the murder investigation, Katie took the opportunity to slip away to the library to retrieve the gift that she had for Mrs. Finch.

When Katie returned to the great room, she was greeted with a chorus of oohs and awes. As Katie presented Mrs. Finch with her gift of the tiny squirming black and white puppy, tears of joy welled up in Mrs. Finch's eyes, and ran down the creases of her little face.

"Katie Scarlett, he looks just like Baby did when he was a puppy."

There was not a dry eye in the place as everyone watched her clasp the small bundle of fur tightly against her chest.

"I figured since George and I are going away on our cruise, you needed someone to keep you company." There was a catch in her voice as Katie uttered these words, and she was desperately trying to control her tears, with very little success.

Ever since Good Old George had decided that it was about time that they took a well-deserved vacation—his little detective needed a well-deserved break away from sleuthing—they had been planning their trip. Katie desperately wanted to get away so that they could have some time together. She had been so consumed with the murder that she had not been taking time to be with her wonderful husband, or for that, matter, to do the things that she so much enjoyed doing. It would be a wonderful time and Katie would try to forget the past couple of months. She would not even think about the murder if she could help it.

To their delight, Joe and Terrie, who now were considered a couple, decided to go with them on the cruise. They would all drive together to Florida, where they would be catching their cruise.

It was a beautiful clear day as they boarded the cruise liner. The sky was so blue that it almost took one's breath away. The suns rays dappled off the ocean and made it appear as if the water was on fire. They were all talking and joking about how they hoped there would not be any trouble on board ship, which would ruin their trip. As they made their way to their cabins, located on the upper deck of the ship, everyone's attention became riveted to the announcement that was being made over the intercom system.

"Welcome aboard," the voice announced. "You are all cordially invited to join us tonight for our Murder Mystery Cruise Dinner. Who out there thinks that they can solve the onboard murder of one of Santa's elves?"

Katie's companions stopped dead in their tracks, and turned to look at her.

George took a deep breath of air and held it.

"Not me," Katie said with a laugh. "My little gray cells are on vacation. George, you'd better keep breathing or I will have to perform mouth to mouth on you," she said this as she reached up and gave him a playful kiss.

As they continued on their way towards their cabin, Katie could not help thinking aloud, "I wonder who in the world would want to murder one of Santa's elves?"

Her query was met with complete silence from her companions.

George finally found his voice and said. "I think that Katie and I will have a nice quiet dinner in our cabin tonight."

Printed in the United States
58427LVS00002B/454-528